THE MYSTERY OF THE CHIMERIC CORNUCOPIA

THE THREE INVESTIGATORS

IN

THE MYSTERY OF THE
CHIMERIC
CORNUCOPIA

BY

ELIZABETH ARTHUR
& STEVEN BAUER

BASED ON CHARACTERS
CREATED BY ROBERT ARTHUR

Hollow Tree Press 2025

CONTENTS

1

A Sticky Beginning

Jupiter Jones leaned over the workbench, focused on bending a small piece of sheet metal into a 90-degree angle. Above him, the six-foot overhang that topped the seven-foot-high fence surrounding the Jones Salvage Yard gave Jupiter plenty of shade from the California summer sun.

This morning, he was making a set of bookends to hold two books he and his friends Pete Crenshaw and Bob Andrews had been given during the course of their last case – a case in which a visit to a movie set had ended with The Three Investigators discovering that a letter apparently written by the famous frontiersman Kit Carson was actually a forgery.

Jupiter was concentrating so hard on both his thoughts and the bookends that he was startled when his Uncle Titus came up behind him and tapped him on the shoulder.

"Jupiter, my boy," his uncle said, reproachfully. "You actually jumped."

"An expected reaction to an unexpected stimulus," Jupiter said. "I suppose it's an evolutionary strategy."

"Speaking of evolution," said Uncle Titus, holding a small manila envelope in front of him in a meaningful manner.

"Quite amusing," Jupiter said – for he knew what the envelope contained. Several days before, he had asked his uncle to retrieve the original of his birth certificate from the safe deposit box.

"I finally got to the bank yesterday," Uncle Titus said.

"Thank you," Jupiter said, reaching for the envelope.

"First, a puzzle for you, my boy," Uncle Titus said, pulling it out of Jupiter's reach. "Twelve children get on a school bus. Everyone on the bus has two backpacks. In each backpack there are two lunch boxes, and in each lunch box there are two apples. How many apples are on the bus?"

He smiled conspiratorially.

Jupiter thought about the puzzle for a moment and couldn't believe his uncle had even given it to him. It was a straightforward problem in mathematics; there was no puzzle about it. Twelve children times two backpacks times two lunch boxes times two apples. Which equaled....

"Wait a minute," Jupiter said. "That's an unfair puzzle."

"Why?" Uncle Titus asked.

"Because you didn't mention the bus driver, who would also be on the bus."

"That's my boy!" Titus said. "Good for you!" He handed Jupiter the envelope. "Now, that's the original – a very valuable document. It's one of a kind. All the rest are simply copies."

It made sense to Jupiter that there was only one original of a birth certificate – because that was also true of the person whose birth it certified. He or she was also one of a kind.

"So be sure to take good care of it," his uncle said.

"I will," Jupiter said.

"You've been very cagey about why you want it," his uncle said. "It's almost like one of those mysteries you and your friends keep solving."

"Not at all," Jupiter said, though he wasn't telling the truth. For several weeks, he'd been wondering about the mystery of his parents – ever since he and Pete and Bob had talked about their families on a case that had taken them to California's Gold Country. The fact was, Jupiter knew next to nothing about his background. His uncle had told him that a many-times-great grandfather had been a coal miner from Wales who had come to California during the Gold Rush, but Jupiter's mother and father had died in a car accident in Canada when Jupiter was just a baby.

"Ever since you told me there's a set of footprints on my birth certificate, I've wanted to see it," Jupiter added.

"I can certainly understand that. You'll never believe how small they are," Uncle Titus said, "particularly given the size of your feet now!" He smiled at Jupiter and went back to his work.

When Jupiter's parents Claudius and Amanda had been killed, Canadian officials had tracked down Jupiter's only known living relative, and a member of the consular service had flown from Toronto to Los Angeles, where Jupiter had been handed to Uncle Titus in a brief ceremony at the Canadian Consulate General.

As it happened, Titus and Claudius Jones had been half-brothers – they shared the same father but had different mothers – and Titus had been almost twenty years old when Claudius was born. On the rare occasions when Jupiter had asked his uncle about his parents, Uncle Titus had been able to tell him very little — even about his father. The two had never lived together and had met and talked only rarely.

At some point, Jupiter had learned that his father had been a professor in the Department of Astronomy and Astrophysics at the University of Toronto, and although Jupiter had no idea what sorts of research his father had engaged in, his uncle had told him that his parents had named him because of something his father discovered about the planet Jupiter and the dynamics of the solar system.

"You're the only person I know," Uncle Titus had told him, "who was named after a planet."

As for Jupiter's mother, all Uncle Titus knew was that she had been born in Sacramento and had grown up in the California Gold Country; that both her parents were Serbian; that she spoke a number of languages; and that her name was Amanda Morris. Uncle Titus had never met her and had only learned the little he knew because he and Claudius had spoken on the phone when their father had died, right around the time Claudius had gotten married.

As soon as his uncle was out of sight, Jupiter put away the tools he'd been using and headed for Headquarters, an old mobile home trailer surrounded by piles of lumber and other salvage that hid it from prying eyes. Several years before, Uncle Titus had given the badly damaged mobile home to Jupiter, and he, Pete, and Bob had fixed the trailer up, brought in a desk, a filing cabinet and bookshelves, and given it several secret entrances so that they could use it as Headquarters for their detective firm The Three Investigators.

Once inside, Jupiter grabbed a white paper bag he'd hidden behind the desk. He'd gotten the supplies in it from Rocky Beach Arts and Crafts in anticipation of his uncle giving him his birth certificate. Now he sat before the fire-scarred desk and put the envelope with his birth certificate and the bag from the art supply store on its surface. Jupiter was expecting Bob and Pete to come over in an hour or two, but, in the meantime, there was a scientific experiment he wanted to conduct – and he wanted to conduct it without them present.

He opened the paper bag and removed a large ink pad with a thin metal flip-top, measuring a foot square, for making linoleum block prints, and a rolled-up sheet of thick white construction paper fastened with a rubber band. The paper was sturdy and textured and designed for printing. Jupiter set these to one side, then opened the envelope his uncle had given him and carefully took out his birth certificate. There in the bottom right-hand corner was a set of baby's footprints – not even three inches long by two inches wide.

Although Jupiter knew that newborn babies couldn't remember their first days on earth, when his uncle had told him his birth certificate had footprints, he'd found it startling to think that one of the very first things that had ever happened to him was having his feet pushed against an ink pad, then pressed on a sheet of paper.

The fact that he remembered nothing about this event had made him skeptical, and that skepticism had bloomed into something larger. What if this birth certificate wasn't his at all? What if that footprint belonged to some other infant entirely? The certificate listed his father's name as Claudius Jones and his mother's name, before she married, as Amanda Morris, and although there was no real reason why his mother's surname couldn't have been Morris, Jupiter knew the name wasn't Serbian.

When he, Pete, and Bob had been up in

the Gold Country, they'd seen a Serbian cemetery at a church in the town of Jackson, and it had been impossible not to notice that the names on the gravestones mostly ended in "ic" or "ich" – names like Vasilovich and Maric and Denisovic and Krzich.

In addition, when The Three Investigators had been in Sonoma on what had become their next case – the one with the Kit Carson forgery – they had met a Serbian boy named Branko Petrovic. In just the last few days, Jupiter and Branko had been exchanging e-mails, and when Jupiter had asked, Branko had told him that two-thirds of all Serbian surnames ended in "ic," just like his did.

Some of them had been Americanized by having an "h" added to the "c," Branko had told Jupiter, but he'd never heard of a Serbian whose last name was Morris. Was it possible, Jupiter had started to wonder, that his birth certificate was a forgery? Since the case on which he and Branko had met had *involved* a forgery, it really wasn't so strange that the question had occurred to him. Luckily, there was an easy way to test this hypothesis.

He quickly untied his right sneaker and took it off, along with his fresh white sock. Then he opened the ink pad and placed it on the floor next to the sheet of unrolled construction paper. He pressed his bare foot against the ink pad – which felt a bit swampy and unpleasant – and then stepped quickly and lightly onto the construction paper. He carefully lifted his foot and held it up behind him.

Hopping around on his left foot, he closed the ink pad and put the paper on the desk. He sat down, and compared the two footprints. They matched almost exactly – allowing for the growth of his foot, of course. He got out his magnifying glass from the desk drawer and studied the two footprints as closely as he could. The whorls and ridges were so similar as to be identical; in fact, he couldn't see a significant difference between them.

Oddly enough, Jupiter felt a little disappointed. It wasn't exactly that he'd been *hoping* his birth certificate had been forged, but he didn't feel reassured to discover that his mother's name had actually been Amanda Morris. Just as he was realizing he hadn't brought any rubbing alcohol to get the ink off his foot, the intercom connecting Headquarters with the rest of the Salvage Yard squawked.

"Jupiter! Are you there?" Aunt Mathilda's voice said. "I'm in the office and the UPS truck just pulled in. There's a package for you, and you have to sign for it. Don't keep the driver waiting."

"I'll be right there," Jupiter said.

Jupiter had a quick, incisive mind, but it abandoned him now as he jumped up, almost lost his balance, and began hopping madly around Headquarters, looking for something he could use to wipe off the ink. He bumped into a chair and grabbed for it, but it was on coasters and almost sent him flying.

Was that a rag on the bookshelf? No, it was a crumpled piece of paper that would do him no good whatsoever.

Out of ideas, he concluded he'd better get outside, so he sat quickly and grimaced as he pulled the white sock over his black-soled foot, then laced up his sneaker. The sock would never be the same, but tough noogies. He scrambled out of Headquarters through Easy Three – its easiest secret entrance – then ran to the office where the big brown truck sat idling.

The UPS man, Billy Wells, didn't seem bothered by having had to wait, but as he pulled out of the Yard, Jupiter's aunt was a bit more stern.

"Heavens, Jupiter," she said. "What kept you?"

"What?" Jupiter said. "Oh, nothing." He was studying the UPS label. "It's from the Petrovics!"

Aunt Mathilda took her glasses off her head and looked at the label herself. "Who?" she asked.

"You know," Jupiter said. "We met Branko Petrovic when we were up in Sonoma, and his parents were so friendly and welcoming. They wanted us to stay for dinner, but we had to leave to meet Pete's father. They're Serbian."

"Well, open it," Aunt Mathilda said.

Jupiter used his Swiss Army knife to cut through the strapping tape. Inside the box he found two very carefully wrapped bottles of wine, one white and one red, and three bars of very fancy chocolate. The label on the wine read Cornucopia Wines, Jackson, California, and featured a straw basket shaped like a horn, with grapes spilling out of it.

"These must be from the vineyard the Petrovics just bought," he said in surprise.

Aunt Mathilda put her glasses back on her head. "That's very thoughtful," she said, "but obviously, these are not meant for you."

"Obviously," Jupiter said. "The wine is for you and Uncle Titus and the chocolate bars are for Pete and Bob and me."

"It's a very nice gift," Aunt Mathilda said.

"From some very nice people," Jupiter said. "Branko's family owned their own vineyard in Serbia, and they came to California about five years ago after Mr. Petrovic was offered a job managing a winery in Sonoma.

"But then he got a better offer in Jackson, and when the owner of that vineyard wanted to sell, Mr. Petrovic bought it. They've sold their vineyard in Serbia and their house in Sonoma and have just moved to Jackson. They waited so long because Mr. Petrovic wanted to make sure his children liked it here before he settled the family down."

"And do they?" Aunt Mathilda asked.

"Yes," Jupiter said. "The Petrovics invited Bob and Pete and me to come visit them in their new place as soon as they were settled."

"Well," Aunt Mathilda said. "I'm impressed. That sort of generosity and friendliness is in short supply these days. Although, actually, you were also lucky with the case you solved for Isabella Chang. I'm still not certain whether I approve of you boys getting such a big reward for finding her gold for her. Enough to put something in all of your college funds and still have enough left over to buy a used car!"

"Yes," Jupiter said. "As soon as the reward comes through, we plan to go car shopping. We're also going to put some money aside to pay Worthington to drive us.

"Did you read the report Bob wrote of our last case?" Jupiter asked, his mind still on Branko Petrovic. "Branko's help was crucial in solving a second case that grew out of it, and he was mentioned not only in Bob's report, but also in some articles in newspapers. He was very excited to see his name in print, and very grateful to us – though really, we're the ones who are grateful to him."

Jupiter turned to see the Salvage Yard's new carpenters, Leif and Magnus, approaching. They were two Norwegian brothers, tall and lean and very blond, and two sides of the same coin. Leif was an optimist, Magnus a pessimist. Aunt Mathilda had hired them to make built-to-order items for the Salvage Yard's customers, and The Three Investigators had commissioned them to build an immigrant's trunk as a thank-you present for a girl named Mallory MacLeod.

Mallory had recently moved to Rocky Beach from Scotland, and she now had a summer job inventorying items in the Salvage Yard. She had helped them on their last case – as well as the one before that – and although Jupiter had been very impressed with the help she'd given them, he found he couldn't quite decide whether he wanted to call her his friend yet. It was true that she was different from any other girl he'd ever known, but that in itself was neither a recommendation nor its opposite.

Still, what *did* recommend her to Jupiter was that she didn't seem to care much what other people thought of her. She also seemed skeptical of received wisdom. And in one of the brief conversations they'd engaged in since his Aunt Mathilda had hired her to inventory and photograph and describe the more interesting objects in the Salvage Yard, she had told him that when she was growing up in Scotland, she had dreamed of being a code-breaker.

Just at that moment, the other two arrived on their bikes. Leif smiled broadly. "I was hoping I'd see the three of you together," he said to Bob and Pete. "We got a call from the artist this morning."

Now that the immigrant's trunk was finished, an artist was painting Mallory's name on it, together with the date she'd arrived in the United States and a lot of boxes holding twining vines and flowers on pedestals.

"She's done her work," Leif said. "I'm sure it's very beautiful."

"We can only hope," Magnus said.

"So we can pick it up in a few days," Leif said.

"If we're lucky," Magnus said.

Bob, whose idea the trunk had originally been, was quite excited but Magnus reminded him never to get too enthusiastic about anything.

Jupiter thought that was Magnus in a nutshell.

"Now get back to work, the two of you," Aunt Mathilda said to Leif and Magnus. "I have a list as long as my arm of customers who want you to build things."

As the brothers left to return to their workshop, Pete laughed. Magnus's gloom always cracked him up.

"Boy, they're funny," he said.

"Like ping and pong," Bob said.

"What's in the box?" Pete asked.

Jupiter pulled out a bottle of red wine from Cornucopia Wines and showed it to his friends.

"Wow," Pete said. "I bet Branko is happy the move is over."

"I expect so," Jupiter said. He grabbed the three chocolate bars and handed one each to Bob and Pete. "See you later, Aunt Mathilda. Come on," he said to his friends.

Jupiter led the way through Easy Three and into Headquarters. They were barely inside before Pete began investigating the chocolate bar's wrappings. But he stopped when he saw the big ink pad and the large piece of paper with Jupiter's footprint on it.

"What's this?" he asked. "An art project?"

"No," Jupiter said reluctantly. "It was an experiment. And I've reached a conclusion. Why don't we all sit down and I'll explain?"

The three of them unwrapped their chocolate and Pete dug in right away. Jupiter broke a small piece off the end of his bar and put it on his tongue. The chocolate was silky and smooth – delicious.

"So," he said. "When Uncle Titus told me that my birth certificate had my footprint as an infant on it, I decided to compare a print I know is mine – this one – " He gestured to the large piece of paper. " – with this one." He showed them his birth certificate, with two small footprints on it.

Pete looked from the footprints to Jupiter's feet and shook his head in disbelief.

"Gosh," Bob said, "those are certainly tiny."

"Ever since we saw St. Sava's Church and especially since we met Branko, I've been trying to make sense of the fact that my mother's name is Amanda Morris. Uncle Titus was quite clear that her parents were Serbian. And Branko was equally clear that Morris is not a Serbian name. So I was sort of hoping that my birth certificate wasn't really my birth certificate, if you follow me. That it was a forgery."

"And what did you find out?" Bob asked.

"The footprints match," Jupiter said. "So I guess it truly *is* my birth certificate and my mother's name really *was* Amanda Morris. But now I'm at a loss as to what to do next to find out more about her. I suppose I might get more information from the University of Toronto. But as of now it's a mystery."

"A mystery for The Three Investigators!" Pete said. His fingers were smeared with chocolate.

"Now, I don't want to drag the two of you into this – " Jupiter began.

"Are you kidding?" Bob said. "I can't imagine a better mystery to solve than the mystery of your past."

"Absolutely," Pete said. "Count us in, one hundred per cent. Jupiter Jones has always been a puzzle, a riddle, and a conundrum."

Jupiter smiled. Pete was quoting from the speech Jupiter always gave when someone wondered what the question marks on The Three Investigators' business card meant. "The question mark is the universal symbol of something unknown," Pete finished, "and Bob and I stand ready to investigate anything. Particularly you." He pointed at Jupiter with a chocolate-smeared finger.

"Tell us what to do and we'll do it," Bob said.

"I'm very grateful," Jupiter said. He felt unexpectedly shy. "Perhaps your mother could help, Bob. Since she's a scientist and has access to those sorts of sites, maybe she could check online to see if there are any scientific papers published by Claudius Jones. It's possible he had a co-author – someone who might still be alive and working in Toronto."

"I'll ask her as soon as I can," Bob said, "and I'll do whatever research I can as well. Could I have a copy of the birth certificate?"

Jupiter quickly made him one on Headquarters' copy machine.

"That reminds me," Bob said. "My mother told me she might call." Bob listened to the messages on his cell phone and Jupiter watched as an expression of excitement flashed across Bob's face.

"Listen to this!" Bob said, when he flipped the phone closed. "We got a call from Isabella Chang. The money she's giving us for finding her gold has been wired into our account! Now we can buy a car!"

"Whoo hoo!" Pete said, jumping to his feet. "That's so great! Let's go car shopping tomorrow. Maybe your uncle could take us, Jupe, since it's going to be registered in his name. My dad offered to help us if he was here, but he's still working on *Bear Valley*."

"I think it would be best if Worthington took us," Jupiter said, "since he's the one who's going to be driving the car for the next few years."

"I'm sure he'll do it," Pete said.

"There's lots to accomplish first," Jupiter said. "We need to send thank-you cards to Ms. Chang and the Petrovics. Bob, maybe you could buy some on the way home." Bob nodded willingly. "And Pete, you can call Worthington and try to persuade him to go car shopping with us."

"Persuade him?" Pete said. "He'll be as excited as we are."

"That may be so," Jupiter said, "but you're excited enough for all four of us."

The three of them left Headquarters through Easy Three in an enthusiastic rush, and Jupiter watched as his friends jumped on their bikes and furiously pedaled away. Three minds were better than one. Jupiter knew he could count on Pete and Bob.

He was lucky to have such friends, and he was even feeling optimistic – more like Leif and less like Magnus – that, with their help, he'd be able to learn something about his parents at long last. He looked down at his right foot. Then he started for the house to scrub off the ink. It would take some doing, but he'd manage it.

2

Three Heads Are Better Than One

The next afternoon, Pete was waiting impatiently near the wrought-iron gates at the entrance to the Salvage Yard when Worthington pulled in, driving his own car. Pete did a double-take. He'd known that Worthington wouldn't be driving the gold-plated Rolls-Royce in which he had driven The Three Investigators for several years, but it was still a shock to see his lanky frame unfold from a compact blue Mini Cooper Countryman – especially one with a white roof, white racing stripes, and white alloy wheels.

"Worthington!" Pete said. He ran over to shake his hand. "What a car! I love it!"

"I think you love all cars, Pete," Worthington said.

"Not *really*," said Pete, blushing. "But this one! It's tiny! And yet somehow big at the same time! I should have known you'd own an English car, but this one is way cool."

"It's a cross between a subcompact and an SUV. They call it an SAV – a sports activity vehicle," Worthington said in his upper-class

British accent. That accent had always given Pete a kick, but he'd found it even more enjoyable ever since Worthington had told The Three Investigators that although he'd been born in Cornwall, England, one of his grandfathers had been from India – a Lascar who had sailed with the British Merchant Marine, then settled in Wales.

Worthington had entered the lives of Jupiter, Pete, and Bob when Jupiter had won the use of the gold-plated Roll-Royce – complete with English chauffeur – by using his powers of observation and analysis to solve a puzzle put forth by the local Rent-'n'-Ride company. It had been a publicity gimmick for the rental agency, but a godsend for The Three Investigators.

Still, it had soon become clear that the Rolls was not as important to the success of their cases as the man who drove it. It had been several weeks since they'd last seen him. After the adventure in which they'd discovered Isabella Chang's gold, their time with the Rent-'n'-Ride had run out. Now, with the money the boys had been given by Isabella Chang, they could buy their own car, keep Worthington as their friend, and hire him, as needed, as their driver. On their last trip together, Worthington had told them he was thinking of going into business for himself, and being among his first customers was a solution that pleased all four of them a great deal.

"Boy!" Pete said. "We need all the advice you can give us about what kind of car to buy."

"Happy to help," Worthington said. "Aside from your sudden wealth, is there anything new in your life since I've seen you?"

"There sure is!" Pete said. "Remember how we rescued that great horned owl up in the Gold Country? Well, I've started working part-time as a volunteer at the Rocky Beach Animal Rescue Center."

"As I expected," Worthington said cheerfully. "You boys never let the grass grow under your feet."

Jupiter and Bob had been in the outdoor workshop, but they now hurried over and shook Worthington's hand, too.

"It's great to see you, Worthington. We've had a whole case come and go since we saw you last. How's everything at the Rent-'n'-Ride?" Bob asked.

"I've started working only part-time," Worthington said. "You'd be surprised how many people still like driving around in an

antique Rolls-Royce. But my boss wants to retire the car, and I see his point. She's a beauty,
but a bit of an anachronism. Besides, I should
be up and running on my own, full-time, in
a month or so. So your reward has come
through at last?"

"Just yesterday," Jupiter said. "And buying a car makes sense, so we don't need to rely
on the Salvage Yard's trucks. Leif drove us into
L.A. on our last case, but we can't make a
habit of asking him or Magnus to help us out
like that."

"My father says we need to be sensible,"
Pete said. "He told me we should look for a car
that'll take us where we need to go − not just
this year or next year, but up until the three of
us go to college. Do you think we should try to
get a Land Rover, like the one you drove us up
to the Gold Country in? I liked how big it was."

"Land Rovers tend to be expensive,"
Worthington said. "Most British cars are. The
only affordable British car is a Mini Cooper.
All the others − Bentleys, Jaguars, Rolls-
Royces, Land Rovers, Aston Martins − they're
all pricey, compared to American cars. I think
your best bet would be to look for something
that has the size of a Land Rover but that's
made by an American carmaker. It would also

make sense to get a car that has either Four-Wheel or All-Wheel Drive."

The boys took their usual places in Worthington's car – Jupiter and Bob in back, and Pete in front, next to Worthington. Snappy and snazzy as the Mini Cooper was, it wasn't as big as it looked, once you got in it. In fact, when you had four people riding in it, it seemed a lot less like an SUV and a lot more like a subcompact.

Jupiter apparently thought so, too. As Worthington left the Salvage Yard, he said, "I didn't realize my legs had gotten so long."

"You've been growing fast," Bob said. "I think you're going to end up a lot taller than you were when we were in junior high school."

"And thinner!" Pete said.

Jupiter fixed him with a gimlet stare.

Everyone was quiet for a moment as Worthington navigated the streets of Rocky Beach. Pete could tell he was heading north, toward the highway.

"Where are we going?" he asked.

Worthington kept his eyes on the road but glanced at Jupiter in the rearview mirror. "I thought we'd start with Freddie."

"Freddie?" Jupiter asked. "You mean 'Freddie's Used Cars'?"

"Exactly," Worthington said. "He's a friend of mine. I have a hunch he'll give us a good deal. Also, he's having a Fourth of July sale."

Pete loved the fact that Worthington said "us." Buying your first car would be exciting for anyone, and under any conditions, but for Pete, it seemed especially great to be doing it with his two best friends and the help of a man like Worthington.

Freddie's Used Cars was on the outskirts of Rocky Beach – a sprawling lot Pete had passed any number of times but never visited. Five minutes later, Worthington and the boys pulled in. The lot was loaded with cars of every color, make, and model, lined up next to one another like horses at the start of a race.

The sun blazed off their shiny polished finishes, sending spears of light in every direction. Their windshields were scrawled with words like "Amazing!" and "Unbelievable!" with prices printed in huge numbers with pink soap. At the center of the lot was a small white wooden building and, over everything, long brilliant rows of pennons, blue and white and red, fluttered in the air. Hanging among these pennons were banners which read FOURTH OF JULY SALE!

They had barely gotten out of Worthington's car when Pete saw a man come striding toward them. He wore a white straw hat and his red face was plastered with a huge grin.

"Worthington!" he shouted.

"Hello, Freddie," said Worthington, shaking his hand. "I think you're in luck today. We're here to buy a car."

Freddie's grin became even wider. "Look around," he said. "Take your time! As you can see, we're having our annual Fourth of July sale. It's pretty busy, so I'll be in the office, but when you're ready to buy, I'll make you a deal you will not believe!"

Pete looked at Jupiter and Bob, who seemed a bit stunned both by Mr. Freddie's enthusiasm and by all the cars – but he himself was more excited than ever. He thought a deal they wouldn't believe would be just the ticket.

"Where do we start?" he asked. "Should we look at them together, or split up? Maybe we could have a sort of treasure hunt. Everyone looks on their own, and then we show the others what we've found." He thought Jupiter would put the kibosh on this idea, but, to his surprise, Jupiter approved it.

"That's a good plan, Pete," he said. "But we must all try to be logical, and not get carried away with emotion. We should buy a car that meets our needs, not a car we love."

"Gee," Pete said. "Can't we get both?"

"Possibly," Jupiter said, "but we have a budget we have to stick to. We also need a car that's big enough to accommodate the four of us comfortably – with room for gear in the back and an extra passenger if needed."

"And Worthington has to like it," Bob said. "We'll not only be asking him to drive the car but to keep it maintained for the next few years."

Pete's eyes were already scanning the rows of cars, waiting for one to call out to him.

There were Kias and Subarus, Land Rovers and Volkswagens, Hyundais and Chevrolets, Buicks and Fords.

"Wow," he said. "How are we ever going to choose? My dad said he likes Fords."

"Everyone check your watches," Jupiter said. "Let's meet back here in half an hour and report."

The four of them took off toward the four corners of the lot. Pete took the southwest corner and started to work his way back in the direction of the building at the center.

At first he was seriously overwhelmed. Almost every car he saw looked great – except for the few that were too old and battered, with body rust or dings in the exterior. But the more he looked, the more picky he felt. He passed by the newer models, with sticker prices thousands of dollars more than their budget. He stayed away from compact cars. And he checked the sheets of paper taped to the windows to make sure they had either Four- or All-Wheel drive.

Pete carefully checked out a Subaru Forester, but it was over ten years old and had over a hundred thousand miles on it. Besides, he thought it was boring. He found a Hyundai Santa Fe, but he hated the color – like coffee with too much cream. Then he saw a car of a sort he'd never seen before in his life. It looked like a Land Rover, but it also looked like a station wagon from the 1960s. A *big* station wagon – and a long one.

It was gray and very boxy, with a black roof, black sidewalls, and a black roof rack. It was weird and different. Pete's heart began to pound. He didn't know exactly why the word "distinctive" popped into his head, or why he would want to own a car you could describe like that, but then he realized that after years of being driven around in a vintage Rolls-Royce, he'd gotten used to being in a car that didn't look like every other car on the road.

The Rolls-Royce had stuck out wherever it showed up, but the great thing about *this* car was that it wouldn't stick out at all. He'd never seen a car exactly like it, but it looked like he *should* have. Maybe best of all, it looked like a car for solving mysteries in. Hector Sebastian – a famous mystery writer the boys knew – was fond of describing The Three Investigators as "gumshoes," and this car looked like a car for gumshoes.

Pete checked the paper describing it. It was called a Ford Flex, and it had All-Wheel Drive and a lot of other cool features. Just like Worthington's Mini Cooper Countryman, it was a crossover – in this case, between a station wagon and an SUV. It also had unbelievably low mileage. And what a price! Pete walked around to the back – and stopped short when he saw a large round decal in the center of the rear window. Below the window, all was gray and sober, but the decal was so colorful it made Pete's eyes pop.

Ever since he'd begun working at the Rocky Beach Animal Rescue Center, he'd encountered animals he'd never seen before, but the creature before him was one he knew would never show up there – or anywhere! It was horrible and awesome at the same time.

It mostly had the body of a rust-colored dragon, with wild serrated wings and tail, its red head scaly and fierce, breathing scarlet fire. But it also had the paws and head of a lion, tawny-coated and roaring, its white incisors gleaming, its black claws tensed.

As if that wasn't enough, it had the head of a ferocious-looking goat as well – its curved yellow horns curling around where its ears should be, and its shaggy white hindquarters, complete with cloven hooves, projecting from the rear. Pete was fascinated. He didn't know what it was, but it sure was *something* – as if a dragon, a lion, and a horned goat had entered the laboratory of a mad scientist who had joined them all together. It was a monster.

But Pete – no fan of monsters – found himself really drawn to it. He loved how clearly each of the three parts was distinctly itself – each fierce and strong, daring all comers. He had the feeling that if the three were shut up in a room together they wouldn't exactly get along. But here, as part of one being, they got along fine. Their fierceness was directed at the world, not at one another – three wildly different animals who had become one.

Pete ran back to join the others. He stood on the gravel lot, his mind racing, and before anyone could say anything, he blurted out, "I found the perfect car. I've never seen one like it. It's boxy, and big, but it has grooves in its doors and tailgate that make it look a bit like a Woodie. You're all going to love it."

As he spoke, he crossed his fingers, because he wasn't as sure as he sounded. If they didn't, he didn't know what he would do. Beg them to buy it, anyway, he guessed. But when he told them the price, Bob's mouth dropped open and Jupiter whistled.

"Outstanding," Jupiter said. "Take us to it."

"There's only one problem," Pete said. "It's not really a problem, though. More like fate."

"What's that?" Jupiter asked.

"It's got a three-headed monster on the back. A decal," Pete said. "Follow me."

He led Jupiter, Bob, and Worthington across the gravel lot, under the hot summer sun, to the Ford Flex. They all looked at it in silence, and then Worthington said, "I see what you mean about the design. It's more sophisticated than most American cars."

"I like the gray and black," Bob said. "And the grooves on the door panels. And those big aluminum wheels."

"It looks very sturdy," said Jupiter. "And you can see at once that it has a lot of storage space. I think this might work very well for us. Good scouting, Pete."

"I knew you'd love it!" he exclaimed. "Come on! You've got to see the decal!" He hurried them over and parked them in front of it.

"It's a chimera," Bob said after a short period of silence.

"A what?" Pete said.

"A chimera," Bob repeated. "A creature from Greek mythology."

"Bob's right," Jupiter said. "But the artist here has taken quite a few liberties. The original had the body of a goat, with the fire-breathing head of a lion, and a snake for a tail. This one is much more elaborate and the dragon comes complete with outspread wings."

"How do you know these things?" Pete asked in amazement.

"Anyway," Jupiter said. "It's not a problem. If we wind up buying this car, we'll just scrape the decal off."

Pete looked at Jupiter as if he'd lost his mind. "Whoa!" he said. "Not so fast."

"I like it, too," Bob said.

"In a strange sort of way, it kind of reminds me of us," said Pete.

"Really?" asked Jupiter. "How?"

"Well, these are three very different animals who all get along. And boy, I wouldn't want to mess with them."

Jupiter smiled. "I see what you mean," he said.

"Of course, I wouldn't want to be the goat," said Pete.

"It's not a goat," Jupiter said. "It's a bighorn sheep. We looked for them that evening we were in Yosemite. Those curved horns are hard as rock. Have you ever seen the males go at it during mating season? I saw it on a nature program on TV. They butt their heads so hard they come off the ground. What a headache! You have to admit, it's an improvement over a standard goat – much more fierce. Your typical *Capra hircus* has fairly straight horns – perhaps a bit curved, but not like that ram."

"Capra what?" Pete asked.

"*Capra hircus*," Jupiter said. "The common goat."

He was about to say more when Pete interrupted.

"Never mind about all that," he said. "Somebody go get Freddie while I stay here and guard the car.”

“This *is* quite a find,” Worthington agreed. “The tires look practically new. The body is in almost perfect condition. And that is exceptionally low mileage for its model year. As for the price – well, it’s more than reasonable.”

With a mounting sense of excitement, Pete danced around the Ford Flex while Bob and Worthington and Jupe walked away and then returned with Freddie.

“I’ve brought the keys,” Freddie said when they arrived. “But don’t get your hopes up. There’s been a lot of interest in that car.”

Pete’s stomach dropped. “That Flex has only been on the lot a day and a half, and you’re the third interested party. I can let you take it for a drive, but one of the earlier cus-tomers put down a deposit, and I’ll need to call both of them before I can offer the car to you.”

Pete had felt like this before, he thought. Usually it happened when his soccer team was on the verge of winning and the opposing team scored a tying goal. Sportscasters called it snatching defeat from the jaws of victory.

Seeing how disappointed Pete looked, Freddie added, “You have a good eye, young man. A lot of people don’t like the way these Flexes look, but the ones who do tend to be crazy about them. Unfortunately, Ford has discontinued the model. They only sold about 20,000 units a year in the whole United States."

Freddie handed Worthington the keys and the four of them got into the car. Freddie's little speech had thrown cold water on their enthusiasm, and Bob and Jupiter were subdued.

But Pete tried to stay optimistic. That decal on the back window was somehow meant to be theirs. Worthington drove a little faster than maybe he should have, to test the brakes and the turning radius. The engine purred, the ride was smooth, and Pete, sitting in the front seat, felt the world coming at him with clarity and immediacy.

"What do you think?" he asked, turning around to look at Jupiter and Bob.

From the smiles on their faces, he knew it was a winner — if they could get it!

Freddie came to meet them as soon as they returned to the lot. Pete couldn't tell from the look on his face what he was going to say.

"I talked to the first interested party," he said. Pete's heart was in his throat. "And he's no longer interested."

"Freddie," Worthington said, and his voice wasn't friendly. "I hope you're not trying to jack up the price of this car."

"William!" Freddie said. "I'm shocked. I have a call into the second party and am expecting to hear – ." The cellphone in his pocket began ringing.

Pete was almost beside himself with anxiety. He tried to calm his breathing but he couldn't and he found he was bouncing on his toes.

"Oh hello," Freddie said. "Thanks for returning the call. The Flex? There's lots of interest. You do? What's that? Tomorrow? Oh, I'm sorry. I can't do that. Maybe some other car?"

The wave of relief that rushed over Pete almost knocked him down. He felt utterly drained, utterly weak. He felt like he needed to sit on the ground.

Freddie hung up. "It's yours if you want it!" he said cheerily.

Worthington was looking a bit peeved as he raised the hood and examined the engine.

"Everything seems to be in order," he said. "However, the car's a bit over our budget."

Pete looked at Bob and both of them looked at Jupiter. All three of them kept a straight face.

"Tell you what," Freddie said. "In honor of the successful conclusion of the American revolution, and because of what I've just put you through, I'll lower the price by $500."

"Freddie, I think you've made a sale," Worthington said.

"Hurray!" Pete yelled. Suddenly he was leaping in the air and pounding Bob and Jupiter on the back. They looked pleased as well, but not as pleased as he was.

When Freddie stepped forward to shake Worthington's hand, Worthington said, "You should shake the boys' hands. They're going to be the owners."

"But I can't sell this car to minors," Freddie said.

"Of course not," Worthington said. "You'll be selling the car to Titus Jones, the owner of Jones Salvage Yard. He's in his fifties, I'd say."

"That's a horse of a different color," Freddie said.

So one by one, and quite formally, Freddie shook Jupiter's hand, and then Bob's, and then Pete's.

"Boy!" Pete said. "I've never owned a car before!"

"You don't own it yet," Jupiter said.

"But consider it sold," he told Freddie. "I'll come tomorrow with my uncle to pay for it, and then he'll register it in his name. Do you, by the way, sell auxiliary equipment?"

Freddie's eyes narrowed. "What did you have in mind?"

"The car already has a roof rack," Jupiter said, "but we'll need a bike rack as well."

"You're in luck!" Freddie said. "Someone bought a car from me the other day which had a bike rack on the back. But he had no use for it, so I removed it. I've got it in the office. I'll throw it in as part of the package."

"Thank you," Jupiter said. "That's very kind. We'll tell everyone we know to buy their cars at Freddie's Used Cars."

"A happy customer," Freddie said, grinning, "is the very best advertisement."

All the way back to the Salvage Yard, Pete was thinking of what a close call it had been. He didn't know what he would have done if they'd lost the car.

They thanked Worthington and said goodbye, then collapsed in the green metal chairs in their outdoor workshop.

"Excitement is often exhausting," Jupiter said. "But it's a good exhaustion."

"Except for the part that wasn't exciting," Pete said.

"Before I forget," Bob said.

Out of his backpack he pulled two thank-you cards – one for Isabella Chang and one for the Petrovics. They each signed their names, and Bob addressed the cards and stamped them, then said he'd drop them in a mailbox on his way home.

"Before you go," Jupiter said. "I was wondering – " He paused and looked off across the Salvage Yard. "Now that we have a car, we should be able to take Branko up on his invitation to visit Cornucopia Wines. I'm a bit embarrassed to admit it, but I've had the funny feeling ever since we passed through Jackson that maybe I could learn something about myself if I were in the town for longer than an hour."

"Bob and I told you our next case was The Mystery of Jupiter Jones!" Pete said.

"That's out of alphabetical order," Bob objected.

"Of course," Jupiter went on, "going to visit Branko just as a way to try to get more information about my mother wouldn't be polite at all. But I genuinely liked him and his family. I think we all did – enough so that even if I knew in advance I wouldn't be able to learn anything while staying with the Petrovics, I'd still want to visit them."

Pete and Bob nodded enthusiastically.

"So," Jupiter asked. "Do you want to go?"

"Absolutely," said Pete, and Bob nodded his head in agreement.

"Good," Jupiter said.

"Well, I'm off," Pete said, getting to his feet. "I want to put in an hour at the Rescue Center."

"I should go, too," Bob said. "If my mom's home, I'm going to ask her to help me figure out how to research scientific articles — and don't worry, even is she isn't, I'll definitely get to it tomorrow."

"What a great day, guys," Pete said. "With a happy ending." He grabbed his bike and straddled it, his feet on the gravel of the Salvage Yard's lot and his hands on the handlebars. "Think of it. Our very own car. A two-toned crossover with a chimera on its back. Here's to us and our three-headed mascot!"

Jupiter and Bob both laughed. As he rode off, Pete called over his shoulder, "Just so long as I don't have to be the goat!"

3

A Very Unusual Galaxy

The following morning, as Bob rode his bike toward the Rocky Beach Public Library, he took his time. For once, he was early. Yesterday had been one of the best days in the history of The Three Investigators, and today Jupiter and his uncle were going to Freddie's Used Cars to pay for the Ford Flex, and then to the Department of Motor Vehicles to register it.

The way Jupiter's mind worked, Bob knew it wouldn't be long before they were off to Jackson to visit Branko Petrovic – the start of a new adventure. Before he'd left the car lot, Bob had taken a picture of the chimera sticker on the Flex with his cellphone. The picture – particularly the ram's head with its impressive horns – had gotten him thinking.

When he'd returned home, he'd done some research, and sure enough, it was as he'd remembered: the cornucopia, or horn of plenty, which adorned the label of the Petrovic's wines, had originally been a goat's horn. And not just any goat's horn.

When Zeus, the greatest god in Greek mythology, had been a baby (with a footprint only a little bigger than Jupiter's!) he'd broken off a horn from the head of a goat attendant, and an endless supply of milk had flowed from it.

Eventually, over time, that horn had become a woven basket and the "plenty" had become an abundance of vegetables and fruits spilling from its mouth.

In America, this image was everywhere at Thanksgiving, on peoples' tables and on supermarket circulars – the traditional depiction and celebration of the harvest.

It was an interesting coincidence, Bob thought, that the name of the Petrovics' vineyard and the sticker on the back of The Three Investigators' new car had both originated in ancient Greece, and both involved a goat.

As he pulled up in front of the library, Bob was dismayed to see that the sidewalk where the bike rack stood was covered with litter – fast food wrappers and napkins, a paper cup, and two empty wine bottles. The neck of one of them had been broken.

Bob glanced at his watch; he still had time. The garbage offended him – both because it upset his sense of order and because it bothered him to think that anyone would be so thoughtless. He supposed that people had started partying early, in anticipation of the Fourth of July. It was just four days away now. Bob dragged a plastic trash can from outside the library's entrance over to the bike rack and began to clean up the mess.

When Mallory MacLeod pulled up on her bike, Bob jumped to his feet, torn between being glad to see her and being embarrassed. They hadn't seen one another since the last time they'd run into each other at the library — just a day or two after The Three Investigators' last case had wrapped. That had begun when Pete's father had invited them to visit the set of a movie he was working on. Later the boys had discovered that Mallory's mother was working on *Bear Valley*, too.

Mallory had helped them with that case — just as she'd helped them with an earlier case in which they'd found a pouch of gold in the floor of the Auburn library — and Bob was frustrated that she didn't yet know about the thank-you present he and Pete and Jupiter were having made for her. Although he wanted to tell her, he knew it would ruin the surprise.

Mallory climbed off her bike and parked. "Good grief," she said. "What a mess." She bent over and picked up one of the broken bottles. "This really takes the biscuit. Not long ago, bottles like these would have been far too valuable to break. They would have been saved and re-used. Not just recycled."

"It's funny you should say that," Bob said. "I was just thinking about cornucopias and the idea that there's an endless supply of something," Bob said. "I like the idea as much as anyone, but there actually isn't an endless supply of anything."

"Why were you thinking about cornucopias?" Mallory asked.

"When Pete and Jupiter and I were up in Sonoma, we met a boy whose parents bought a vineyard called Cornucopia Wines."

"You mean Branko Petrovic?" Mallory asked. "I heard Jupiter talking with Pete about him the day the four of us went to Los Angeles."

"That's right," Bob said. "His family raised some special varietal of grape back in Serbia."

"In Scotland, it's mostly whiskey," Mallory said. "Although, in Orkney there's a company that specializes in fruit and vegetable wines. My father used to drink them."

Bob swept together the broken glass with a napkin, grabbed the last of the paper and deposited it in the trash can, then returned it to the library's entrance. Mallory locked her bike to the rack and scraped some small shards of glass off the edge of the sidewalk with her shoe.

Bob came to stand beside her as she struggled out of her backpack. His hands were sticky and he held them out to the side, not sure what to do with them.

"So what's new with you?" Mallory asked.

Now, Bob felt even worse that he couldn't tell her about the immigrant's trunk, because his biggest news was that the money from the Li Chang case had finally come through. He saw no way around mentioning it, so he did. Then he told Mallory that he and Pete and Jupe had gone car shopping, and that the car they'd chosen had a decal of a chimera on its back. He felt almost certain she'd know what a chimera was, and he was right.

"One of those mythological creatures with the head of a goat?" she asked.

"Exactly," Bob said. "We don't think about goats as being very important these days. But they were probably quite important in ancient cultures."

"Let's see," Mallory said. "What do I

know about goats?"

She paused, thinking. "Well, in the Old Testament, the Jewish chief priest would take the sins of the people and lay them on a goat – symbolically, of course – and then cast the goat out into the wilderness."

"The poor goat," Bob said.

"Yes," Mallory agreed, "but it supposedly removed all the peoples' sins. Hence, scapegoating."

"Wow," Bob said. "I didn't know that's where the word came from." Mallory continued to impress him. "So what's new with you? Has your house in Scotland sold yet?"

"No," Mallory said. "Not yet. But I'm getting to like living in the Wessex House. I've also met a girl I think I'm going to be friends with."

"That's great. Who is she?" Bob asked.

"She's in your grade," Mallory said. "Our grade, I guess. Califia García-Williams. She said she knew you and Jupiter and Pete."

"Everyone knows Pete and Jupiter," Bob said. "I know Califia, but not too well. She's in the dance and theater clubs. She hangs out mostly with those kids."

Mallory nodded. "Because that's what she loves; her mom's a dancer and her father's an actor. He's playing a Spaniard in *Bear Valley*. My mother took me to the set the other day, and Califia was there, visiting her father."

"Gosh," Bob said. "Of course! The movie is still filming. It's almost like I thought it had stopped because The Three Investigators were no longer connected to it."

Mallory laughed. "Anyway, she was friendly and funny, and I liked her father, too. She invited me to go swimming with her sometime soon."

"See," Bob said. "I told you to give Rocky Beach a chance."

"I *have* to," said Mallory. "For two years, at least. Anyway, that's the deal I made with my mother."

There was a pause while they smiled at each other. Bob couldn't believe how easy it was to talk to Mallory, but then he glanced at his watch.

"Holy moly," he said. "I thought I had all the time in the world, and now I'm late!"

Bob grabbed his backpack and Mallory grabbed hers and together they mounted the steps to the library. "You're here to get more books?" he asked as he held open the door for her and Mallory breezed through.

"Yes," Mallory said. "I just finished

Treasure Island."

"Did you like it?" Bob asked.

"Parts of it," Mallory said. "I couldn't believe I'd never read it before. I found it in the children's section, but it really isn't a children's book. And the part about the ship breaking loose is just a *tiny* bit implausible."

"I know," said Bob. "But I liked the action at the Admiral Benbow. I'll see you later." Bob smiled and strode off toward the Men's Room, even though he saw Miss Bennett standing in the door to her office – looking, he thought, just a bit stern. Mallory headed for the Circulation Desk.

Bob washed his hands quickly, then hurried to Miss Bennett's office. Although he expected a word about his tardiness, she merely gave him his tasks for the morning.

Amazingly enough, she didn't want him to shelve books. He was to water the small trees and shrubs in the stone planters; they were arrayed along the sunny windows in front of the reading desks and gave the library a semitropical air – the philodendron and the palm, the bromeliad and the ficus. At ten o'clock, she wanted him to stand guard over the Circulation desk, and, if he could find the time, to work on the newsletter.

He was on his way to fill the watering can when he saw Mallory leaving. He waved to her, and she waved back.

The time went quickly – the library was crowded this morning, with lots of people returning and checking out books – and before Bob knew it, his shift was over. On his ride home, he thought about Mallory, about how good it had been to see her, about how happy she'd be (he hoped!) with the immigrant's trunk. And he thought about her new acquaintance, Califia García-Williams.

Truth be told, Bob had always been a bit intimidated by Califia. Like him, she had mixed parentage; her father was Hispanic and her mother African-American. Her skin was light copper; she looked perpetually sun-kissed, and she had amazing curly hair. She also had a great deal of self-confidence, and he especially remembered how, in sixth-grade English, Califia had astonished him and the other students.

The teacher had asked everyone in the class to memorize a poem and then to recite it to a school-wide assembly. Almost everyone chose a short and simple poem. But not Califia. Bob couldn't recall what she had recited, but he remembered that when she was finished, there wasn't a sound in the auditorium; in fact, it seemed everyone had stopped breathing. And then everyone started hooting and yelling and applauding and calling her name. He was sure Califia was a terrific actress.

When he got home, Bob put his bike away in the garage, ran inside, and made himself a sandwich. His mother hadn't had time to help him with his Claudius Jones research the night before, and when he discovered that she'd been called into the laboratory at the college where she taught, Bob turned to his father.

"Sure," Mr. Andrews said. "I can help." Because of his work as a journalist, Bob's father had access to special scholarly and scientific sites not open to the general public. "But first," he suggested, "why don't we check out the department where Jupiter's father taught?"

In Bob's father's office, the two of them sat in front of the desk, and Bob's father booted up his desktop computer. Mr. Andrews opened the University of Toronto's website, then navigated to the Department of Astronomy and Astrophysics.

"Hmm," Mr. Andrews said. "Very cutting edge." It turned out that members of the department were engaged in research on stars, galaxies, quasars, clusters of galaxies, and problems in general relativity.

"What's a quasar?" Bob asked his father.

Mr. Andrews laughed. "Do I look like an astrophysicist? From what I understand, it's a really big and really far away something or other in the sky that gives off huge amounts of energy and probably is filled with black holes. Does that satisfy you?"

Bob grinned. "Sure," he said. "Thanks. At least we know Jupiter's father was interested in stuff we can't understand."

It didn't take long for Mr. Andrews to begin to uncover footnotes and citations in articles, and he followed links and chased down leads until he opened a summary – called an "abstract" – of a paper that Dr. Claudius Jones, Ph.D., University of Toronto, had written. In it, Dr. Jones detailed the discovery of a previously undiscovered and very unusual galaxy. Dr. Jones had named the galaxy "Xandra" – though that wasn't its official name.

As far as Mr. Andrews could tell, the scientific literature was absolutely flooded with citations regarding the paper. Bob's father explained that this was significant; it meant that other scientists and astrophysicists had found Dr. Jones's paper important – even ground-breaking. In science, the more citations, the better. But it turned out Claudius Jones had written the paper alone; Jupiter would be disappointed to learn there was no co-author.

"I wonder what Xandra means," Bob said.

"Let's look it up," his father said.

And that's how Bob discovered that *Xandra* was the nickname for the Serbian girl's name *Aleksandrina*. Bob thanked his father for his help, and with his heart pounding harder than usual, went up to his own room. He wanted to get on his laptop and look into all of this further. Was it possible that Jupiter's father had named the galaxy after his wife, and that Jupiter's mother's name was really Aleksandrina, not Amanda at all?

It was strange enough to think that Jupiter really *had* a mother and father, and that they'd been totally different from Aunt Mathilda and Uncle Titus. He reached in his backpack and took out the copy of the birth certificate that Jupiter had given to him, then set it next to his open laptop.

Since Bob had had great luck with an online genealogy site when he'd done research on Isabella Chang's ancestor Li Chang, he'd been planning to use the site again ever since Jupiter had asked for Bob's help with researching his parents. It had turned out to be a very handy resource for finding out more about people, since the site linked you directly to multiple public records and other sources of information.

However, the first time he'd used it, he'd simply signed up for a one-week free trial. Now that the free trial had come to an end, Bob decided to subscribe to the website – paying a month at a time. In a few keystrokes, he was in, the subscription paid for by The Three Investigators' PayPal account, set up several years before to pay for things like this.

The minute he was in, Bob was invited to open a page on which to construct a family tree, and since it made sense to start with what he knew to be true, Bob typed in Jupiter's name and his birth date, then, above him, the name of his father, Claudius Jones, and his date of birth.

After that, he turned to Jupiter's mother. In the proper spot next to her husband, he typed "Amanda Morris" and her date of birth. Sure enough, in a few moments he was linked to a public records page affirming that

Amanda Morris had been born on that day in Sacramento, California.

But before Bob could remember what he knew about Jupiter's father's side of the family, a window popped up, asking if he wanted to examine Amanda Morris's death certificate. That was strange. Puzzled, he clicked "Yes" and was taken to another public records page where he could see for himself that the Amanda Morris born in Sacramento on Jupiter's mother's birthday had also died there five years later.

This stunned Bob. Obviously it couldn't be right. Whoever Jupiter's mother might have been, she clearly hadn't died at the age of five – and also, she had died in Canada. On a whim he typed the name Aleksandrina Morris into the website's search engine but found no relevant records. He then tried Aleksandrina Jones, Xandra Jones, and Xandra Morris, with the same result.

Increasingly frustrated, Bob remembered that on his last case, when he had been looking for a man named John Lysander Smith, he'd had no luck in finding him until he typed the word "Lysander" all by itself. That had been a lesson that sometimes, with the Internet, less was more, so now he searched for

"Aleksandrina," born in California, on the date on Jupiter's birth certificate.

Within seconds, the screen lit up. He'd discovered the birth certificate of a girl born in Jackson, California, on the same day as Jupiter's mother. Her name was Aleksandrina Markovic, and her own mother was a woman named Nadja Dimitrijevic; her father was Spiridon Markovic. The back of Bob's neck prickled and he almost forgot to breathe.

The genealogy website was fascinating. The more you discovered, the more suggestions it gave you. It asked you question after question, leading you to more and more information, guiding you into the past as the history of a particular family began to reveal itself bit by bit. But it was also opaque and inscrutable at times – with frustrating blanks, omissions in the public records, empty spaces with no clue as to how to fill them in.

Bob got lost in the process, but as he filled in some of the blanks and added names, he couldn't help noticing that the family tree he was constructing was large at the top and kept narrowing until it arrived at a single name at the bottom – Jupiter Jones.

It was an upside-down triangle, with Jupiter's possible ancestors spilling toward the bottom, and with Jupiter himself at the very tip – an odd and pleasing coincidence, in which the growing family was like a horn of plenty.

Although Bob had no idea whether Aleksandrina Markovic was actually Jupiter's mother, every time he was asked if someone should be added to the tree he said "Yes."

Through this process, he discovered that Nadja's grandfather was named Dranko – born in 1897, in what was now Serbia – and that he had emigrated to the United States after World War I.

There were no documents linked to Dranko Dimitrijevic except for census records and telephone books, but when Bob turned to Aleksandrina Markovic's *father's* side, he discovered a whole lot more information. Xandra's father Spiridon had been born in a displaced persons camp in Yugoslavia in 1945, Bob read. His parents had been ripped from their home by the Second World War, and after it had ended, they had come to America in 1947 – when Xandra's father was two.

Bob did some more general research online and discovered that Xandra's father's parents (born in the early 1920s) must have come to the United States seeking asylum — political refugees who feared persecution by the Yugoslavian Communist government.

This information about Xandra's grandparents gave Bob a strong fellow feeling, because his *own* grandparents (on his mother's side) had fled to America from China in order to escape persecution during Mao Zedong's Cultural Revolution.

But there was plenty more to discover. Bob kept following suggestions the website gave him. He soon found that Xandra's father's parents had journeyed across the United States and had landed in Jackson, California, with its Serbian enclave.

There, in 1969, when Xandra's father Spiridon was only 24, he had bought a small vineyard. Bob read that he had named the vineyard "Dragutin Wines." It seemed that "Dragutin" meant "precious" in Serbian. Unfortunately, Xandra's father had died of a heart attack at the age of 50, and some time afterward, Dragutin Wines had been sold to a man named Michael Ivan.

Bob hoped that the Dragutin Wines website would have a history of the vineyard – with full details about the Markovic family – but when he opened it, he found no history.

That was strange, Bob thought, because Dragutin seemed like the kind of vineyard that people traveled quite a distance to visit. Its website was very fancy – filled with gorgeous photographs of wine and wine bottles and grapes and tasting sheds and pergolas and walkways.

Bob supposed that if people actually *went* to Dragutin, the owner might tell them more, but he could discover nothing useful on the website itself. One thing did amaze him, though; when he clicked on the Google maps link, he found that Dragutin Wines and Cornucopia Wines shared a property line. They were neighbors.

Wow! thought Bob. That was really great. Now that they were going to Jackson to visit Branko, he, Jupiter, and Pete could do research on the ground. Maybe they could even meet Michael Ivan, the man who owned Dragutin Wines these days – Branko's parents must know him – and ask him what he knew about the Markovics.

Bob grimaced. So far, all of this was just conjecture, a wild fantasy fueled by a single coincidence – that Amanda Morris, of Sacramento, and Aleksandrina Markovic, of Jackson, had been born on the same day. Everything else could well be a figment of Bob's imagination – as well as a series of prompts and suggestions that some computer program had offered him.

It had gotten late in the afternoon. His mother would be home soon from the lab. Even now, the smells of food being prepared in the kitchen were drifting up the stairs; his father seemed to have started dinner. He'd ask his parents about all of this while they ate. But right now he wanted to talk to Jupiter.

With his fingers crossed, Bob dialed the number of the landline in Headquarters. It rang a few times and then Jupiter picked up.

"Three Investigators Headquarters," Jupe said. "Jupiter Jones speaking."

"We investigate anything," Bob said.

"Bob!" Jupe said. "I'm glad you called! I paid for the car, and Uncle Titus and I registered it this afternoon. A two-toned Ford Flex with a chimera on its back window is parked right behind the office. I'm putting the bike rack on later."

"That's terrific," Bob said. "I have some news as well. My head's spinning from all the details, so I'll let you make sense of it."

He started at the beginning, with a description of the work being done in the Department of Astronomy and Astrophysics. Then he moved on to the academic paper written by

Dr. Claudius Jones concerning the discovery of a galaxy he'd named Xandra.

"I found out that Xandra is the nickname of the Serbian name Aleksandrina," Bob said. "And then I discovered that a woman named Aleksandrina Markovic was born in Jackson on your mother's birthday."

"You mean Amanda Morris's birthday?" Jupiter asked.

"Yes," Bob said.

"The same month, the same day, the same year?" Jupiter asked.

"Yes," Bob said. "Identical. That's the whole point. Amanda Morris and Aleksandrina Markovic were born on the very same day. But it's even stranger. Really weird."

"Go on," Jupiter said. Through the telephone, Bob could almost hear Jupiter's brain whirring.

"Amanda Morris? I found her birth certificate online. But I also found her death certificate. According to the public records, she died when she was five."

There was a long silence on the other end of the line.

"Jupe?" Bob said. "Are you still there?"

"I certainly am," said Jupiter. "That's very interesting information, Records."

4

A Timely Invitation

Two days later, Jupiter and his friends were all up by 6:00 in order to get on the road to Branko's family's vineyard by 7:30. Twice before – and in less than a month – they'd taken this same highway north – once to Auburn and once to Sonoma. But while the route was familiar, the experience of driving on it was entirely different – because *this* time, Jupiter thought, The Three Investigators were riding in their very own car.

Jupiter looked out the tinted window of the Ford Flex as The Three Investigators sped up Interstate 5 toward Cornucopia Wines – their gear securely stashed in the back, their bikes fastened to the bike rack. Along with their personal gear was another bag, filled with equipment The Three Investigators used for special sorts of investigations – strong flashlights, headlamps, and a sturdy coil of rope, among other things. Branko had mentioned there was a cave on the property.

"How great is this?" Pete said from the front seat, next to Worthington. "You sure got things organized in a hurry, Jupe!"

Jupiter shrugged, trying to appear nonchalant. "Once I could visualize our objective, it wasn't hard to move forward. Of course, it helped that Branko and his family were so eager to have us join them for the Fourth of July. Apparently this is the first year they've been invited to Dragutin Wines' annual fireworks celebration."

"Anyway, you know that Jupiter has never had any patience for delays," Bob added.

True enough, Jupiter thought. When he had the bit between his teeth, he ran hard. It had been less than a week since the wine and chocolate had arrived from Branko Petrovic's parents.

After buying and registering the Flex and getting the startling news from Bob about his research, Jupiter had called Branko, and the vague invitation they'd been given when The Three Investigators had first met the Petrovics had become specific:

"Come as soon as you can! We've been invited to our next-door neighbor's annual party!"

Jupiter, who prided himself on his generally self-possessed and calm demeanor, had been so excited that he'd hardly been able to sleep at night. He'd paced his bedroom floor, his mind racing. Bob had told him not only that Amanda Morris and Aleksandrina Markovic shared a birthday, but that Amanda Morris had died when she was five. And it hadn't escaped his attention that the two girls shared the initials A.M.

Jupiter hadn't mentioned it to Pete or Bob yet, but he knew for a fact that one of the best ways to erase your old identity and find a new one was to obtain a copy of the birth certificate of a baby who'd been born on the same approximate date as you, but who then had died quite young.

Of course, now that documents like birth certificates and death certificates were all being made available for scrutiny online, the time was undoubtedly coming when it would be impossible to do this successfully. However, it hadn't been impossible in the 1980s and 1990s. Still, if Xandra Markovic had been his mother, why had she wanted to disappear?

Jupiter was quite surprised at himself. He felt jumpy, keyed up, eager to get to Jackson. He was determined to get to the bottom of whatever mystery presented itself. After all of the cases he'd solved with detachment and logic, he had stumbled on one that was intensely and immediately personal.

Everyone but him was relaxed and happy. Worthington whistled from time to time and Pete talked about the black bear with mange who he'd more or less adopted at the Animal Rescue Center. And they couldn't stop talking about the Flex; they were all absolutely smitten with their car.

This was their first long trip in it, and everything about it was perfect. Worthington and Pete were happy up front, with a console between them, and the back seat was spacious, with more than enough room for him and Bob. The ride was smooth – comparable to the Land Rover. Jupiter knew they'd made the right decision; the Flex met their needs seamlessly.

Still, Jupiter thought, they'd wanted a car with a generally low profile, unlike the Rolls. While he agreed with Pete that the two-toned black and gray station wagon, with aluminum alloy wheels, looked like a car that one of Raymond Chandler's gumshoes might have liked, the colorful winged creature plastered across the back window would certainly stick out in any crowd.

Even so, Jupiter was already fond of it. It was just as dramatic as any of the scenes or animals painted on the Salvage Yard's fence, and he was starting to think Pete had been right when he'd said it almost seemed like fate for their new car to have it on the back. After all, how many creatures from Greek mythology had the heads of three different animals?

Also, chimeric, as an adjective, meant illusory, fictitious, imaginary, misleading, or fanciful, and every case The Three Investigators had ever solved had involved at least one moment when they had encountered something chimeric. That was why Jupiter's skill at deductive reasoning was so important.

Something that at first appeared fantastic had always proven to have a logical explanation, and if you argued backwards from that premise, at least you were on solid ground. Deductive reasoning required you to make sure your premises were correct before you drew any conclusions.

"You know, I've been thinking," Pete said. "This will be the first time the three of us have ever celebrated the Fourth of July anywhere but at home in Rocky Beach!"

"I don't suppose the Dragutin fireworks will be as extensive as the ones at home, but I bet the setting is a lot more picturesque than the football field at the high school," Jupiter said. "And I'm glad the Petrovics invited Worthington to drive back up and join us on the night."

"I'm looking toward to it," said Worthington. "If I didn't have to work tomorrow, I wouldn't even drive back south in the meantime."

"The fireworks are at a very fancy vineyard, so they might be bigger than you'd think," Bob said. "And besides, there'll be plenty of excitement when Jupiter dances the kolo."

Pete started laughing, and when Worthington asked, Bob explained: when they'd met the Petrovics, Mr. Petrovic had told Jupiter that, when the boys visited, they'd have a Serbian celebration with Serbian dances.

Pete wiggled in his seat, constrained by his seat belt, and snapped his fingers.

"Calm down, Pete," Jupiter said. "Whatever the kolo is, I'm sure it's not the Mexican hat dance."

Now everyone burst out laughing and it was several minutes before quiet resumed.

"Worthington, I meant to ask you," Bob said. "When were you a chauffeur for that rich man in Jackson?"

"That was almost twenty years ago

now," Worthington said.

"While you were there," Bob asked, "do you remember a local story about a big counterfeiter getting arrested?"

"No," Worthington said. "I can't say I remember anything like that."

"Why are you asking?" Pete said.

"Before we left this morning," Bob said, "I asked my dad if he knew anything about the town of Jackson. He said that in the mid-1990s the F.B.I. and Secret Service arrested a guy named André Laurent there. He was French-Canadian and had originally lived just outside of Boston. I think that's why it stuck in my dad's head − because his family lived nearby. The F.B.I. and the Secret Service almost caught André Laurent back east, but he ran at the last minute. He even killed his partner − the guy who had made the engraving plates. He took the plates, then stabbed his partner in the heart."

"Wow," Pete said. "He sounds like a real nice guy."

"They got him in Jackson," Bob said, "but he skipped bail. He was never tried and never re-arrested. I had about a half hour to look up some articles about him. It seems the authorities never found the press he must have used to print his counterfeit money."

"Geez," Pete said. "They never found André Laurent's printing press? And he vanished completely before he was tried? I thought that crime didn't pay." He turned around to get a better look at his friends.

"Money is so weird," he went on. "Everyone has to have it, but it's only fancy paper, isn't it?"

"It used to be backed with gold," Jupiter said. "Paper bills are all about credit, based on the idea of trust and good will, but gold and other precious metals have inherent value. That's why Li Chang's gold was still worth a lot of money a hundred years after he hid it. On paper, it was actually worth *more* than it had been in his day. Theoretically it should have been able to buy the same amount of stuff, but it's worth was greater because of inflation."

"Inflation makes my head ache," said Pete.

"All paper money is essentially illusory," Jupiter said. "We agree you can buy a certain number of jellybeans with a dollar, and so when you go to the candy store, you expect a certain number of jellybeans."

"But next year," Pete said, "you can expect fewer."

"That's inflation," Jupiter said. "When things rise in value, and the same amount of money buys less every year."

"I bet I could spend my whole life studying," Pete said, "and I'd never understand economics. Every time I think I'm getting something, I'm not."

"That might be because even top economists disagree about what makes an economy work – though they do agree that low inflation is very important," Jupiter said.

Jupiter always enjoyed a conversation about ideas, but he found he was less interested in what had started it – a story about a counterfeiter who had vanished twenty-five years earlier. It seemed hardly likely to have any impact on their trip.

Unless, of course, he thought with a smile, André Laurent had returned to the scene of the crime and was busily at it, making fake bills again. North of Stockton, Worthington left the interstate and headed east toward Jackson. They were all more quiet now; the long trip had hypnotized them – the thud of tires, the world flashing by at a constant speed.

But once they were in wine country, Jupiter roused himself, and by the time they passed the intricate hand-carved wooden sign for Cornucopia Wines – a woven basket spilling grapes – and were bumping down the long gravel driveway to the house where the Petrovics lived, he was fully awake.

On either side of the drive, rows of grapevines stretched as far as Jupiter could see, row after row, their serrated leaves lushly green, clusters of still-small, still-green grapes beginning to hang on their stems. Their grasping tendrils made curlicues against the deep blue sky and held tight to the heavy wire strung along the rows, between the individual vines – which had now begun to grow into one another, almost as if they were joining hands.

The air was dry but perfumed, and the boys rolled their windows down. In the distance they could hear a dog barking.

Normally Jupiter was not all that receptive to beautiful landscapes, but this one was truly striking, and also timeless. Human beings had been making and drinking wine for many thousands of years and had cultivated and tended vineyards like this one for over five centuries.

Perhaps, Jupiter thought, growing up right next to a salvage yard had dulled his sensitivity to the beauty of the natural world. The closer they got to the main house, the more vibrant everything seemed. There were brilliant borders of flowers, and ornamental trees, and, in a gravel circle before the front door, a statue of a young boy with a jug in his hand from which water constantly flowed. Chickens who had been pecking at the driveway scattered before the Flex, clucking madly.

They had barely come to a stop when Branko Petrovic burst from the front door. He looked just as he had in Sonoma – tall, lean, muscular, wiry, and electric with energy. When Jupiter got out, Branko ran up to him, his dark eyes gleaming. He looked very tan, and his helmet of bristly black hair gave him an unusually intense look.

"Jupiter!" he said, shaking Jupiter's hand. He turned to welcome Pete and Bob.

"And this is our friend Worthington," Jupiter said.

"Mr. Worthington," Branko said. "The pleasure is mine. Come inside, all of you."

Jupiter looked at Worthington who shook his head briefly, and Jupiter decided it wasn't worth it to get Branko to drop the "mister."

They were barely inside the front door when a whirlwind met them. Branko's younger brother and sister, Zivko and Milena, came rushing in, yelling. If they had been cautious in Sonoma, they had thrown caution to the winds. They collided with Pete in a great flurry of screams and laughter, almost knocking him over. Though Branko tried to act displeased, the younger children's enthusiasm was infectious, and the warm welcome continued as Mr. and Mrs. Petrovic came into the entrance hall from wherever they had been.

Jupiter couldn't believe how different the house was from the Arts and Crafts house the family had owned in Sonoma. While that had seemed a bit hushed and dim and elegant, this was whitewashed and flooded with light. The high ceilings seemed to reflect the day, and all the Petrovics' furniture and the other belongings were transformed here – more casual and sun-spangled and welcoming.

"Come in, come in," Mrs. Petrovic said. "You must all be exhausted. Mr. Worthington, what can I get you?"

They followed Mrs. Petrovic to the kitchen – everyone but Pete, who was dragged outside by Milena and Zivko to meet their dog, Zeus. Children always seemed to like Pete, and he always seemed to like them, Jupiter thought. In the kitchen, he saw a big farm table laden with food.

"We'll be eating in an hour and a half!" Mrs. Petrovic said.

Jupiter looked at his watch. It was 12:30. They'd made good time. But when Worthington said he had to drive back to Rocky Beach right away, Mrs. Petrovic, after exhorting him to stay, made him a sack of sandwiches.

"We'll see you again on Sunday!" she said.

The Petrovics joined Bob and Jupiter as they went outside to say goodbye to Worthington. Jupiter caught sight of Pete; he was in the side yard, throwing a tennis ball for Zeus, a young white Lab.

Each time he threw it, Zivko and Milena were convulsed with laughter, because Zeus would start off after the ball and then get sidetracked and begin nosing around in the shrubbery. Pete would go and retrieve the ball and try again.

Jupiter and Bob unfastened their bikes and Pete's from the bike rack, and then Worthington raised the hatchback and unloaded the boys' gear. Just before Worthington got back in the Flex, he took a critical look at the car. Their passage had whipped up the dust of the roads near the vineyard and now it coated the exterior.

"I'll leave the Flex at the Salvage Yard," he told Jupiter as Pete came running up, a bit out of breath. "I'll make sure I wash the grime off before I come back for the Fourth of July."

Then he was in the car and off down the driveway. Jupiter, Pete, and Bob stood waving until the Flex was just a speck in the distance.

"All right," Branko said. "Come see where we are staying!"

"It's a little, how you say, rustic?" Mr. Petrovic said. "But I think you boys will like it." He looked at his watch. "Now, Branko, do not run out of time. Please bring your friends back by 2:00. We eat then."

Jupiter picked up his gear and followed Branko who took the boys down a small lane to an outbuilding about a hundred yards from the main house.

"The man Papa bought the vineyard from," Branko said cheerfully, "had wine tastings here once. But now every year during the harvest, grape pickers come and sleep."

The building was an old single story made of wood, clapboard-sided, with a shingled roof, whitewashed like the house. In front was a stone patio under a steep overhang that shielded it from the evening sun.

"This is so fantastic!" said Pete. "It's like

having our own private clubhouse."

Jupiter couldn't have agreed more. Inside was a large room, off of which were two smaller rooms with bunks built into the walls. There were also two bathrooms.

"Look," Branko said. "We can all sleep in one room. There are eight bunks. We can each sleep on a lower bunk if we want."

"You're going to sleep out here with us?" Pete asked.

"Yes," Branko said. "I have permission."

"That's so great, Branko," Bob said. "Now we can really get to know you."

"What's that green light?" Pete asked, pointing to a device on a table near the front window. "It looks like a router."

"It is," Branko said, "so the bunkhouse gets Wi-Fi."

"Wow!" Bob said. "We can use my laptop out here."

The boys went to one of the smaller rooms and unpacked. Jupiter picked the lower bunk closest to the door; he'd feel more comfortable there. While Pete and Bob were finishing unpacking, Jupiter wandered back into the main room.

On the walls were framed posters, advertisements, and photographs featuring Cornucopia Wines. Among them were a number of now-yellowing newspaper articles clipped from the pages before being matted and framed. Most were about wine and vineyard-related events in and around Jackson.

Jupiter examined them closely. When Bob wandered into the room, Jupiter called him over. "Look at this!" he said enthusiastically. He pointed to an article with a photo attached. In the photo were two men identified as Spiridon Markovic and Mihailo Ivanisevic.

"Wow!" Bob said. "That's Xandra's father," he said, pointing to Spiridon Markovic.

The article was dated 1990 and concerned the expansion of Dragutin Wines. Jupiter remembered that Dragutin shared a property line with Branko's parents' vineyard. The other man in the photo, Mihailo Ivanisevic, was the loan officer at the bank that was extending the capital for the expansion.

The article was filled with overly-hearty quotes from both men, praising one another and their Serbian roots. Ivanisevic was quoted as saying he had total confidence in Spiridon Marcovic and in the future of winemaking in Amador County.

Another framed article hung next to the first. This one had a picture of a young girl standing between a man and a woman before a pickup truck filled with trugs overflowing with grapes. The caption identified the trio as Spiridon and Nadja Markovic and their daughter Xandra. Dragutin Wines was celebrating a record harvest and had been nominated as Vineyard of the Year.

Jupiter checked the date on the article – September 1991. Xandra would have been eight. The young girl looked exceedingly proud and happy. How amazing, Jupiter thought, that this eight-year-old might have grown up to be his mother. He squinted, looking closely to see if he could discern a resemblance.

Still, as much as he might want the two of them to be mother and son, why would someone who had grown up on what seemed to be quite a successful vineyard have changed her name and moved to Toronto, Canada – or wherever it was she'd met Jupiter's father?

Branko and Pete came out of the bedroom, horsing around. They were about the same height, and Jupiter thought it was nice to see his old friend and his new friend together – one so bright and sunny and given to bursts of enthusiasm, the other so polite at first, and formal. But now it was Branko who seemed carefree and enthusiastic.

"Come," he said. "There is much to show you before we eat."

Branko took them on a brisk tour of the vineyard. He showed them the shed where the grapes were pressed, the vats where the juice was collected, and the huge barrels in which the wine was aged. He took them at a breakneck pace down a row of vines, explaining about pruning and harvesting. Jupiter could have gotten lost in the vines, and his head swam with the sights and smells, the feel of the dirt underfoot, and the rough leaves against his arms.

"And now the best!" Branko said. "This way to the wine cave!"

Behind a large wooden door, Jupiter found himself in a man-made cave that had been dug into the side of a hill. It was dim inside, and cool. The arched ceiling rose high above their heads, and huge wooden barrels, like the ones Jupiter had seen earlier, lined the walls.

"This is where the grape juice becomes wine," Branko explained. "It is cool here and stays at a constant temperature, and the humidity is high, all good for the wine."

"Who built this?" Pete asked.

"I do not know for sure," Branko said.

"One of the earlier owners. There are many wine caves in California – though more in Sonoma where we used to live than here."

"I think winemakers sometimes use real caves, don't they?" Pete asked.

"I am sure they did in the past," Branko said. "But now they are all constructed for the special purpose." He looked at Pete slyly. "If you like, tomorrow we can explore the real cave."

"That would be great!" Pete said.

"It's at the top of our vineyard, right on the edge of our property – near the line separating us from Dragutin Wines. I have not yet been inside, except to see that it really *is* a cave. On the map it looks as if there is also an entrance on the other side of the property line."

"Like a secret passage between the two vineyards!" Pete said. "We can explore it together. We brought our flashlights and headlamps and a rope."

On the way back toward the main house, Jupiter was thinking about the events of the morning. He had enjoyed the drive and the arrival, and it had been nice of Worthington to suggest giving the Flex a good wash before he came back.

The decal of the chimera suddenly came

to mind. All at once Jupiter felt very protective of it. He didn't yet know if he wanted to leave the decal in place, but he certainly didn't want it removed by accident or mistake. He felt the need to call Worthington and tell him to please be careful – to make sure that, if he washed the car, he didn't damage the decal.

As it was almost time for lunch, Branko led them to the main house. Worthington was still on his way back to southern California, and Jupiter didn't want to call him on his cell-phone and disturb him mid-trip. He decided to call his aunt and ask her to tell Worthington about the sticker when he got back to the Salvage Yard.

"Do you think I could use your parents' phone to call my aunt?" Jupiter asked Branko.

"Of course!" Branko said. "Come with me." He took Jupiter to a private alcove where he could make the call.

Jupiter thanked Branko, then dialed the number of the Salvage Yard's office. His aunt should still be there. The phone rang three times, and then a voice said, "Jones Salvage Yard. Can I help you?"

To Jupiter's surprise, the voice was Mallory MacLeod's.

"Mallory," Jupiter said. "It's Jupiter."

"Jupiter!" Mallory said. "Is everything O.K.?"

"Yes," Jupiter said. "I was expecting to reach my aunt. Is she around?"

"She was, but I don't see her now. I was just dealing with Skinny. He stopped by to invite me and my mother to a Fourth of July party at his house, and I was so eager to tell him I'd rather spend it in a closet that I didn't notice where your aunt went. Sorry."

Skinny Norris was Mallory's first cousin but had long been a thorn in the side of The Three Investigators. Jupiter wasn't surprised she was trying to avoid spending time with him.

"Can you give my aunt a message when you see her?" Jupiter asked.

"Sure," said Mallory.

"We're with Branko Petrovic in Jackson. Everything's fine, but Worthington is driving our new car back to the Salvage Yard right now. Please make sure my aunt tells him there's no need to wash the car, but if he does, to be careful not to damage the decal."

"Do you mean the chimera?" Mallory asked.

"Yes," Jupiter said. "How do you know about that?"

"Bob told me about it. I saw him at the library. I'll be sure to tell your aunt – or Worthington, if I see him first. By the way, I liked him a lot when I met him that day up in Auburn. I liked Leif, too, when he drove us to Los Angeles, but he seems very shy around girls. He told me to tell you the project is finished."

"The project? What project?" Jupiter asked.

"He didn't say. He just said 'the project,' and giggled a lot," Mallory said.

Of course! thought Jupiter. The reason Leif seemed shy around Mallory was that he and his brother had been trying to keep her from seeing the immigrant's trunk they were building. Jupiter felt like an idiot for having said *The project? What project?*

"Maybe Bob knows what it is," Jupiter lied.

So the trunk was finally finished, he thought. And right before the Fourth of July. There was something quite pleasing about the coincidence, and to his own enormous surprise, Jupiter suddenly found himself saying, "As it happens, Worthington is coming back to Jackson for the Fourth. We've been invited to some fireworks at a nearby vineyard. If you'd like to join us, you could get a ride with Worthington in our new car."

"Gosh," Mallory said. "I'd have really liked to come, but my mother's already accepted an invitation for both of us from a man she met on the set of *Bear Valley*."

Jupiter didn't know if he was glad or disappointed, but he got off the phone as quickly as possible after that, half-wishing he hadn't asked her at all, but half-glad he hadn't nipped his own hospitable impulse in the bud.

5

California, Cornucopia of the World

Back in Rocky Beach, it was about four hours later, and although Mallory had been working hard ever since Jupiter's phone call, she hadn't been able to stop thinking about it. She'd never spoken to Jupiter on the phone before, and his voice had sounded less expansive and all-knowing than it did in person. He'd even sounded flustered and unsure of himself when she'd given him Leif's message. She'd been surprised by that, but she'd been flabbergasted when he'd invited her to join The Three Investigators on her first Fourth of July in California. She was sorry she hadn't been able to say yes.

As it turned out, when Jupiter had called the Salvage Yard, his Aunt Mathilda had been off on an errand, and when Mallory had gone looking, Mr. Jones had told her that his wife wouldn't be back until 4:00 or so. At 6:00, Califia García-Williams was coming to the Salvage Yard to take Mallory to her house to go swimming. So Mallory had decided to work until she arrived – sorting, describing, and putting stickers on a number of framed reproductions of advertisements from the 19th century she'd discovered in one of the sheds.

As she worked, she kept thinking of Jupiter's Fourth of July invitation. The last time she'd been with The Three Investigators, she'd done something really dumb; she'd forgotten to tell them that a homicidal maniac involved in the case they were working on would soon be released from jail. In the end, it hadn't mattered, but even so, she'd felt really embarrassed. For one thing, her memory was usually excellent, and for another, ever since she'd met Bob, Pete, and Jupiter, she'd been wishing she could sometimes work with them on their cases. It wasn't just that she liked each of the boys separately; it was that she liked them as a *unit*.

Mallory had never made new friends easily, and although she'd had boy friends as well as girl friends back in Scotland, the boys she'd been friends with hadn't been friends with one another first – not the kind of friends Pete and Bob and Jupiter were.

As she thought, Mallory was sitting cross-legged on the floor, sorting and labeling the 19th-century advertisements, with their deep saturated colors and unusual designs. There were advertisements for oranges and grapefruits and other fruits and vegetables which had been grown in California, and advertisements for things that had been shipped in from places in Australia – mangoes and kiwi fruit. But now Mallory had come across an advertisement for California itself.

She looked closely at the information in the corner and found that the poster was a blowup of a pamphlet put out by the Southern Pacific Railroad in 1888. Its background was a rich, almost burgundy red on which were emblazoned the words CALIFORNIA, CORNUCOPIA OF THE WORLD in bold white letters. Given that The Three Investigators were currently visiting the Cornucopia Vineyard, her discovery of this poster might be seen as quite a coincidence, Mallory supposed, if cornucopias weren't such a common symbol.

As it was, what interested and amazed her was that, although California was now overrun with people, only a hundred and thirty years ago the Southern Pacific Railroad had had to persuade people to emigrate to the state. At the time, there had been almost forty-four million undeveloped acres of land there.

Across the left-hand side of the poster, a straw-colored basket in the shape of a horn stood almost on end, spilling flowers and bananas as well as peaches, oranges, grapes, plums, and a pineapple. Across the right, spreading toward the bottom, was the copy:

Room For Millions of Immigrants
43,795,000 Acres of Government Lands Untaken
Railroad and Private Land for a Million Farmers
A Climate For Health and Wealth
Without Cyclones or Blizzards.

It was a description of paradise – though with a decidedly practical bent – and whoever had written it could never have imagined how overburdened with houses and cars that paradise would eventually become. Bob had been right when he'd said there really wasn't an endless supply of anything, Mallory thought. People wanted there to be, of course – and not just because they wanted plenty, but because they wanted *certainty*. A guarantee that the way things were now was the way they would stay. When Mallory's father had died so unexpectedly, she herself had discovered, once and for all, that no matter how you might long for a world like that, it didn't exist.

Even so, there was something about the Southern Pacific Railroad's pamphlet that made the late 19th century seem like an era of extraordinary optimism. In fact, the advertisement evoked the era in which it was written more effectively than a lot of textbooks did, and also seemed an excellent reminder of the importance of not judging the past by the standards of the present.

Mallory was trying to write copy for it when Mrs. Jones mounted the wooden steps and stood in the doorway of the shed she was working in.

"Hello, my dear," she said. "Anything exciting happen when I was gone?"

Although something exciting certainly *had* happened, Mallory looked up and said, "Not really. Jupiter called from Jackson."

"Did he?" Mrs. Jones asked. "Is everything all right?"

"Yes," Mallory said. "He wanted me to tell you that Worthington would be bringing their new car back this afternoon. And for somebody to tell him there's no need to wash the car, but if he does, to please be careful not to damage the decal on the back."

"That's a lot of fuss about a three-headed monster," Mrs. Jones said. "But I presume Jupiter knows what he's doing."

"He also invited me up to Jackson," Mallory said, almost blurting it out − as surprised to be telling Mrs. Jones as she'd been to get the invitation in the first place.

"Land sakes," Mrs. Jones said. "It's getting harder and harder to keep track of you young people these days."

Mallory smiled.

"I can't go. My mother's already accepted an invitation for both of us to go to a picnic and fireworks with a man she just met at work," she said.

"I absolutely *love* fireworks," Mrs. Jones said. "And wherever you're going, it should be a treat for you. I doubt there are many Fourth of July celebrations in Scotland."

Though this was true enough, Mallory felt the need to stick up for her father's country.

"No," she said. "But we do have Burns Night."

"Burns night?" Mrs. Jones said, looking at her quizzically. "That sounds downright dangerous. What in good heavens is that?"

"It's January 25th," Mallory said, "and it's a celebration of the Scottish poet Robert Burns. On his birthday."

"With fireworks?" Mrs. Jones asked.

"No," Mallory admitted. "With a dinner." She paused. "With a haggis." Her defense of Scotland wasn't turning out that well, she thought.

"In America, it's apple pie and ice cream on July 4th. Also a lot of whooping and hollering at saying goodbye forever to King George," Mrs. Jones said. "Though I'm afraid not too many people think about that any more." Coming to stand beside Mallory, she peered down at the advertisement for California, then picked it up to look at it more closely, clucking her tongue.

"Can you imagine?" she asked Mallory. "California has forty million people living in it now, but back then, they had to advertise to get people to move here. At least there are still no blizzards, thank heavens. Except in the mountains."

"I was thinking the same thing," Mallory said. "Well, not about the blizzards but about how much has changed in the last hundred and thirty years." Then she surprised herself again by saying, "Do you think I could buy this poster out of my pay?"

"Of course you can buy it!" Mrs. Jones said. "And in the spirit of the Fourth of July, I'll give you 20% off. Just set it aside in a corner and stop trying to write copy for it. You've already found its new owner!" She smiled at

Mallory and Mallory smiled back.

If she'd been asked, Mallory couldn't have told Jupiter's aunt exactly why she wanted the advertisement, but she knew that when she had time to think about it, she'd figure it out. In the meantime, she went to a table holding a roll of red and white SOLD stickers and slapped one just below the words CALIFORNIA, CORNUCOPIA OF THE WORLD.

At that moment, both she and Mrs. Jones heard the sound of wheels crunching gravel, and Mallory peered out the window to see Worthington pull up next to the office in what she guessed must be The Three Investigators' new car. She thought it was strange-looking, but a lot less garish than a gold-plated Rolls-Royce.

"Worthington's here," she told Mrs. Jones.

"Well, let's give him Jupiter's message," Mrs. Jones said, leading the way outside. As they came up beside him, Worthington was stretching his lanky frame.

"Hello, William," Mrs. Jones said. Mallory looked at her in surprise. She smiled. "You didn't think that for all these years I was going to call this man by his last name, did you?" she said.

Worthington said, "Good afternoon, Mathilda. Always good to see you."

"Hi, Worthington," Mallory said, a bit self-consciously. "Jupiter called to say you'd be bringing the car back."

"And something about being careful of that terrible monster decal," Mrs. Jones said, "if you wash the car."

All three of them stepped to the back of the car and studied the chimera. Since Mallory had never before seen the car, she'd also never seen the chimera, and she thought it was delightful – delightfully antic, delightfully colorful, delightfully powerful. She also saw at once why Jupiter and the other boys had liked it.

"I quite understand," Worthington said. "I think the boys are becoming fond of their three-headed mascot."

"This young lady just told me that Jupiter invited her to join them for the Fourth," said Mrs. Jones. "If she didn't have somewhere else to go that night, I imagine she'd be riding up to Jackson with you on Sunday."

"Jupiter asked you to join us for the Fourth?" Worthington said. "I'm surprised. The boys are pretty friendly, but The Three Investigators as a trio keep to themselves. You must have magical powers."

Mallory found herself almost blushing. She hardly ever did – not really – but when she got confused enough, she had a horrible feeling that she might.

Worthington looked at her. "I apologize for my flippant comment. What I meant to say is that I've always known that the boys had good taste, and that I'm sorry I won't be able to enjoy your company. After all, we ex-pats must stick together."

At this, Mallory felt much calmer. Although she didn't want to start thinking of herself as an *ex*-resident of Scotland, it was sweet of Worthington to acknowledge that both he and she had arrived in California from the United Kingdom.

"Thank you, Worthington," she said.

He then turned to Mrs. Jones.

"Mathilda," he asked, "where would you like me to park the boys' car?"

Mrs. Jones looked around the lot. "Land sakes," she said. "It doesn't really matter. Why not under that tree where you left your car?"

Worthington nodded and got back in the Flex. Mallory and Mrs. Jones watched him as he parked and got into his own car. He sped off, waving as he went.

"He's brilliant," Mallory said.

"I bless my stars every day that he was the chauffeur who came with the Rolls-Royce," Mathilda said. "Now I've lost track of time. You finish up in there. I have to go start Titus's supper. Would you like to join us?"

"No, thank you," Mallory said. "That's really nice of you, but a friend of mine is going to stop by and pick me up when I'm finished working."

"Pick you up?" Mrs. Jones asked. "Now don't make me worry about you."

"A girl from my class," Mallory explained. "Jupiter, Pete, and Bob all know her. She's coming by on her bike to take me swimming at her house."

"That's fine, then," Mrs. Jones said. "Just make sure you close the main gate when you leave."

She smiled kindly at Mallory and walked off toward the back of the lot. Mallory watched her go. She was becoming more and more fond of Mrs. Jones. She went back to the office and continued her work.

Mallory had only met Califia once, and she was looking forward to seeing her again. She had a quiet self-confidence, a grace, and a subdued friendliness that Mallory found appealing. She also seemed philosophical somehow – even wise – and though Mallory knew that she herself was very smart, she sometimes feared she lacked wisdom and was hoping to figure out how to get some.

Out in the yard, she heard the clatter of a bicycle and by the time she'd gotten up and through the door of the shed, Califia had started up the steps. She was a little shorter than Mallory, with a lithe taut dancer's body and a coiled energy that registered as optimism. Her dark hair was curly, there was lots of it, and she seemed perpetually happy – though not at all pushy about it. She radiated good will and friendliness.

"Hi, Mallory," she said.

"So you had no trouble finding me," Mallory said.

Califia smiled. "Everyone in Rocky Beach knows the Salvage Yard," she said. "The home of Jupiter Jones."

"I didn't know he was *that* famous," said Mallory.

"I wouldn't say he's famous," Califia said. "But he's well-known. He's the brainiest kid in the class, and his friend Pete Crenshaw is great. He can be a bit rambunctious, but he's funny and he's got a really big heart. I know Bob the least well. How did you meet them?"

"I was riding by the Salvage Yard one day," Mallory said, "and they'd put a suit of armor in the entrance as a joke. One thing led to another and I got mixed up in their last two cases."

"Including the one which started with the movie my father's working on," said Califia, smiling.

Up until now, she and Mallory had been standing in the doorway of the shed, but now Mallory said, "Before we take off, do you want to see where *I* work?"

"Sure," said Califia, so Mallory led the way inside and showed her the pile of framed advertisements she'd been writing copy for, and then decided to show her the California advertisement that now leaned against the wall with a SOLD sticker on it.

"Look at this," she said. "Can you believe that there was a time when they had to *advertise* for people to move to California?"

As she pulled the poster out and held it up, she also found herself saying, in some surprise, "You know, Califia and California are actually pretty similar."

"It's a little embarrassing," said Califia, "but we're both named after the same fictional character."

"I bet you've told this story a million times," Mallory said.

"I have," Califia said. "But I don't mind. It's complicated, though. Why don't we get on our bikes, and I can tell you about it on the way to my house?

"Just let me sign out," Mallory said. She found the clipboard with her time sheet on it and wrote the time down. Then she grabbed the backpack with her swimsuit and a towel and closed the door of the shed behind her. She and Califia each retrieved their bicycles, and when they'd rolled them through the entrance to the Salvage Yard, Mallory carefully closed the wrought-iron gates.

"Ready?" Califia said, buckling on her helmet.

"All set," Mallory said. Back in Scotland, she'd never worn a helmet and had been very surprised to learn that, in California, everyone under seventeen was supposed to wear one. She intended to avoid it as long as possible.

They both started pedaling, and after a while Califia started talking. "To answer your question, Califia was a black pagan warrior queen in a Spanish novel written around 1500. She lived on a made-up island named California. The island was named after the queen, and when Spanish explorers discovered Baja, they thought *California* would be a good name for it – because they thought Baja was an island."

Mallory could understand that. Baja California was a long and skinny peninsula between the Pacific Ocean and the Bay of Cortez, off the coast of Mexico. Anyone could be excused for mistaking it for an island, she thought.

"So my Hispanic father and African-American mother decided it would be cool to name me Califia. I like it," Califia said, "but sometimes I wish they'd named me something simpler, so I didn't feel I had to live up to such a fancy historical name."

"I know what you mean," Mallory said. "I give thanks my parents didn't name me Boudicca. Still, Califia suits you."

Actually, Mallory had often wished her parents *had* named her Boudicca – a real warrior queen, not a fictional one – but she didn't think she should say this to someone she was still just getting to know. Also, a lot of bad things had happened to Boudicca, Mallory reflected.

It didn't take long to get to Califia's

house – a multilevel house with a single-pitch roof, which rose in the back. The front was sided with stone and redwood and had large windows. A tall fence started at the rear of the property and surrounded the backyard – where the pool was. They leaned their bikes against the side of the house and went through a gate in a tall rose arbor. The backyard was terraced with stone and timbers holding grasses and shrubs, with the shining lozenge of the pool at the center. From behind, the house was a wall of glass opening on the pool.

Califia took Mallory to the small pool house at one end where they changed into their suits. By the time Mallory came out, Califia was poised on the pool's edge. She dove gracefully into the water, and Mallory followed her.

The water was cool, and it felt silky against her skin. She swam underwater for half the pool's length and then surfaced and swam to the far end. After several laps, she just floated on her back and let her legs dangle. Above her, the sky was blue, cloudless, darkening as the evening came on.

After a while, she and Califia climbed out and toweled off. The sun was lowering in the west, no longer visible from Califia's back yard. The two of them sat in canvas slingback chairs near the pool's edge.

"That was great," Mallory said. "If you'd ever swum in a Scottish loch, you'd know how great."

"I take it the water's cold."

"Everything's cold in Scotland," Mallory said. "They've just discovered central heating."

Califia laughed. "You have a great sense of humor. No wonder The Three Investigators like you."

"Thanks," Mallory said. She didn't normally think of herself as having a good sense of humor – or *any* sense of humor, really – but she enjoyed the compliment.

"Anyway, I'm not sure they *do* like me. I was just in the right place at the right time. Twice. I helped discover a map that led them to that hidden gold up in Auburn, and a week ago or so I posed as a history buff to get a copy of a forged letter from its forger. Amazingly enough, I pulled it off."

"Maybe you should join the Drama Club," Califia said, smiling.

"I'm not an actress. Or actor, as I guess they're calling them nowadays," Mallory said.

"I actually like 'actress' better," Califia said. "I can see renaming 'mankind' as 'humankind', but not everything has to be gender-neutral. Just because 'authoress' has always been an insult doesn't mean that 'actress' has."

"I completely agree with you," Mallory said. "You said you'd been cast in a play this summer?"

"*Romeo and Juliet*," Califia answered. "I'm playing Juliet in the Rocky Beach Summer Theater Festival. Every summer they put on four productions, and they cast Equity actors as well as amateurs. We're so close to L.A. they can do that. An Equity actor is playing Romeo. He's seventeen, I think. I have a crush on him, actually. I'm sure I'll get over it."

She laughed easily and naturally as she said this – a perfect example of her wisdom, Mallory thought.

"I've never had a crush on anyone," Mallory said. "I tend to get crushes on ideas or things or books. Or words. I love words. I love Shakespeare."

"You'll have to come to a rehearsal, then," Califia said. "Or maybe you could get a job on the crew or something. By the way, are you doing anything for the Fourth of July?"

"My mother and I were invited by a guy she met on the set of *Bear Valley*," Mallory said.

"I'm actually a little bummed. Pete and Bob and Jupiter are visiting a vineyard in Jackson called Cornucopia Wines, and out of the blue Jupiter asked me if I wanted to join them."

"Wow," Califia said. "That's very cool. I don't know why you said you're not sure they really like you. Are they solving a mystery up there?"

"I don't know," Mallory said. "But mysteries seem to pop up wherever they go. You could say they live in a cornucopia stuffed with mysteries."

Califia laughed again, and Mallory thought back to the moment she had put the SOLD sticker below the words CALIFORNIA, CORNUCOPIA OF THE WORLD. When she'd asked Jupiter's aunt if she could buy it, she hadn't known why she wanted it, but now she did. She wanted to give it to The Three Investigators – not right away, but when she knew them a little better.

After all, both Three Investigators' cases she'd been involved with had had the history of California in the 19th century at their centers. Also, Mallory thought, if anyone would understand her reflection about people wanting *certainties*, it was Jupiter Jones, Bob Andrews, and Pete Crenshaw.

6

A Secret Lair

The next morning was Saturday, July 3rd, and up in Jackson, The Three Investigators and Branko planned to go caving. As Pete sat under a tree in the back yard of Branko's house, he was shoveling food into his mouth while he thought about his checkered history with caves. Although Pete *liked* caves – at least in theory – it seemed as if every time The Three Investigators went *near* a cave, something bad happened. It was almost spooky, and although Pete tried hard not to be superstitious, he wasn't always successful.

He regularly carried a secret rabbit's foot in his pocket on Three Investigators cases. At home he kept a lucky horseshoe beside his bed, and, of course, he never *ever* walked underneath a ladder and always threw salt over his left shoulder if he accidentally spilled it. In fact, he was throwing salt over his shoulder right at this very moment, as he and Pete and Jupiter sat with Branko and the Petrovics at an outside table, eating breakfast.

Pete had been awakened early by

Branko, who kept poking him on the shoulder and hissing "Pete!" close to his ear. He grumbled, but when he saw Branko's delighted face, he decided to wake up, and the two of them slipped into their clothes and crept out of the bunkhouse. By the time Jupiter and Bob had joined them, yawning and rubbing their eyes, Pete and Branko had been invited to sit down with Mr. Petrovic and Zivko, while Mrs. Petrovic and Milena hurried back and forth from the kitchen.

When Pete asked if he could help, Branko said, "Yes, but at some other meal. Mama wants this special for you."

It *was* special, too. There were baked eggs and fresh bread and a platter of thick-cut tomatoes sprinkled with fresh basil. Pete had been putting a little salt on his tomatoes when he had spilled some and tossed a pinch of it over his shoulder. Now his mouth watered as Mrs. Petrovic placed a large round pastry in front of Branko's father, and Mr. Petrovic began cutting wedges and passing them to the boys.

"This is called burek," he said. "A Serbian specialty."

Pete took a bite. "It's really great!" he said.

Mrs. Petrovic smiled indulgently. "You are a fine boy," she said. "You eat everything on your plate. But why did you throw salt over your shoulder? To blind the devil?"

To blind the devil? Was *that* why he was doing it? Pete thought, feeling a bit alarmed. And if so, what the devil was the devil doing behind his shoulder, anyway?

"I hope not!" he said. "My mom's a little superstitious, and when we do things like go caving, I get superstitious, too. But I actually don't know what the salt thing is all about."

Beside him, Jupiter stirred. "In ancient times, salt was expensive – so precious that, in some civilizations, it was even used as currency," he said. "I believe the logic of the original custom was that spilling salt was like throwing away money, and that only the devil could make someone act so foolishly."

"Salt was *money?*" asked Pete.

"As valuable as gold," Jupiter said. He, too, seemed to be enjoying the burek. "It was used to preserve meat and animal skins, and also to flavor food."

"At least in the hands of a cook as good as my wife!" Mr. Petrovic said. "But why does caving make you superstitious, Pete?"

That, too, was a tough question, Pete

thought – and this time, it was Bob who answered it.

"I don't think it actually makes him superstitious," he said. "It's just that the last time we stayed in a vineyard, he and I ended up having to hide in a cave while we were being chased by some men who wanted to steal a string of pearls. The pearls were stashed in a big old-fashioned flashlight, and Pete ended up putting the flashlight in a burro's skull just before he got captured."

Pete appreciated Bob's help, but he wished he hadn't mentioned the burro's skull. The whole thing had ended, *that* time, with Pete being grabbed by a bad guy as he emerged from the dark of the cave into the light of day.

"I understand," said Mr. Petrovic. "But our cave is just a cave."

"I don't think we should let them go!" said Mrs. Petrovic, suddenly agitated. "What if something happens?"

"Don't worry," said Jupiter smoothly. "We have ropes and flashlights and headlamps. We also have whistles and walkie-talkies. Cellphones don't work in caves, but walkie-talkies work quite often. We'll be careful. We always are."

"Remember, Mama," said Branko.

"These are The Three Investigators!"

Pete found Branko's faith in them genuinely reassuring. So, apparently, did Branko's father, because as Zivko fed Zeus little bits of burek, Mr. Petrovic said, "That reminds me. Last night, there was a break-in!"

Pete turned his attention from the food. Bob and Jupiter were looking expectantly at Mr. Petrovic.

"Where?" Branko asked.

"Right next door at Dragutin," Mr. Petrovic said. "Michael Ivan called this morning to tell us that when he and Sarah got up, they found that their wine cave had been broken into. We know them from St. Sava's. Michael said that nothing was taken, but the door was damaged and they will have to get it repaired."

Branko looked stricken. "I am very sorry for the Ivans," he said, "but will there still be fireworks? I promised my friends."

Mr. Petrovic laughed. "Yes," he said. "I am sure the intruder did not steal the fireworks. Though I do not know what he was looking for. A barrel of wine? It does not make sense."

"Have there been any other break-ins in the area?" Jupiter asked.

"No," Mrs. Petrovic said. She crossed

herself. "And may that be the last."

"Michael Ivan has owned Dragutin for many years," Mr. Petrovic said, "but he has not many friends – except for people he knows through church. He loves the church more than almost anything – though the party he holds every year on the Fourth of July is also for his neighbors."

"He seems very successful," Mrs. Petrovic added.

"There is a rumor that the man who owned the vineyard before Michael ran into money problems," Mr. Petrovic explained.

"You mean Spiridon Markovic?" Jupiter asked.

"Yes!" Mr. Petrovic said. "How do you know this?"

"There's a newspaper article on the wall of the grape pickers' shed," Jupiter said. "About Spiridon Markovic borrowing money from a local banker to expand his operations."

"Of course," said Mr. Petrovic. "Now, remember that we will have a cookout tonight with the Pelletiers. So you boys should be back here by five o'clock to welcome our guests. We will eat at six."

Pete was so full he couldn't imagine ever eating again. At dinner the night before, Mrs.

Petrovic had served so much food, Pete had felt it was only polite to keep filling his plate. And now he'd had a third helping of the burek.

"What will you have for lunch?" Mrs. Petrovic asked.

Pete groaned.

"Wait here," she said, and soon returned with a gigantic bag of sandwiches, fruit, and bottled water for the boys to take with them on their caving expedition.

As Pete and the other boys walked back toward the shed, Bob asked, "Who are the Pelletiers?"

"They are friends of my parents," Branko said. "When my father was managing Cornucopia Wines before he bought the vineyard, Mr. Cooper, the owner, hired Mr. Pelletier. He is a management consultant and he and my father got along well. Also, his children are friends of my brother and sister."

Back at the shed, they quickly loaded their gear – and the food and water – into their backpacks. From the Three Investigators duffel, they each took a powerful flashlight and a headlamp. Luckily there was an extra of each for Branko. They decided they wouldn't take the rope, since if they encountered any situation in which they might need it, they would simply turn around and come back. This was a sort of reconnaissance expedition.

"You really *are* prepared!" Branko said.

"We try not to go anywhere without being well-equipped," Jupiter said, with a touch of pride. "Second, Records, make sure you have your chalk and your walkie-talkies."

"What is the chalk for?" asked Branko.

"We each have a different color," Jupiter said, "and when we need to mark a trail, or leave a sign that we've been somewhere, we draw a question mark. My color used to be white, but red is more easily seen from a distance. Like salt and gold, red is a rarity in nature."

That was the kind of observation Jupiter was always making. At least Pete was getting better at understanding animals! He hoped there were bats in the cave. Someone had just brought an injured bat to the Rescue Center, and Pete had learned a bit about it. There were twenty-five separate bat species native to California, and luckily white nose syndrome − which had killed a lot of bats back east − had not taken hold in California yet.

The cave was some distance from the shed. They walked through what seemed to Pete like a mile of grapevines − a long straight tunnel with green leafy sides, but with the brilliant pure-blue dome of the sky overhead. When they reached uncultivated land in a corner of the property, Pete noticed the tracks of white-tailed deer and something he thought must have been a raccoon. The ground became uneven and rocky and began to rise in elevation.

"Look!" Branko said, pointing, and Pete and his friends followed Branko's finger. Up ahead, where there was an unusual hilly formation, Pete saw a dark shape, which could only be the mouth of the cave.

It got bigger the closer they got to it, and when they finally arrived, they found the cave mouth large enough so that all four of them could comfortably stand up in it. Ahead of them the cavern narrowed, but it was still wide and high for as far back as Pete could see.

"We should put our headlamps on," Jupiter said. "And I'm getting out my compass." After unzipping and then rezipping his backpack, he held a compass up in one hand and a piece of red chalk in the other.

"Sometimes the old ways are best," he said. "A magnetic compass works fine underground – unlike a GPS which relies on satellites. I think we should work our way east-northeast as best we can. Before we entered, I checked, and that seemed the proper direction if the cave has entrances from both vineyards. I'll mark the route with a question mark every ten or fifteen feet."

"Good thinking, Jupe!" Pete said. "Even if we can't get through to the other side, we'll be able to find our way back out again."

As they edged in, the concentrated beam of Pete's headlamp, now fastened to his forehead, followed his gaze wherever he looked – over the sandy floor beneath his feet, into the darkness of the two tunnels leading off the cavern.

So far at least, the place seemed like a normal cave, but Pete was reserving judgment until they got farther inside. Jupiter led and Branko went next as the boys moved on into the larger of the tunnels. They moved slowly, and it seemed to Pete that every minute or so Branko looked back at him with a big grin on his face. Branko was so excited! Pete thought. He didn't think he'd ever met anyone quite like him.

As they left daylight behind, the light from their headlamps bounced off the walls in crazy unexpected ways, strobelike, making Pete a bit dizzy. The air was cool and smelled of earth and stone. He was surprised at how many twists and turns the cave took, and how many side channels there were. Every few minutes, Jupiter came to a branching of two tunnels. It would be easy to get lost if you weren't marking your route with chalk, Pete thought.

By now, they had switched their flashlights on, and the illumination dwarfed the light from the headlamps. They'd been walking for about fifteen minutes when they passed a small cavern on their right and decided to explore it. It was really *very* small – maybe twenty by twenty – but it had unusual nooks and crevices in its rocky walls. Pete found one that would have been perfect for hiding something – so perfect he felt sure, for a minute, that something *must* be hidden in it.

However, there was nothing – though he still called the others over to see the interesting formation.

"It's almost as good as the secret drawer in John Chang's house," Pete exclaimed admiringly. "Except that it doesn't slide in and out, of course!"

Jupiter didn't use his chalk inside the little chamber, but when they returned to the main tunnel, he started leaving red question marks

again. To the left, to the right, to the left again
– the route was almost dizzyingly complex,
Pete thought.

Then, all of a sudden, they entered a
large interior chamber. By now, they'd been
walking for almost thirty minutes, and as they
emerged into the chamber, the air seemed to
Pete to smell different.

Jupiter thought so, too. "I'd say we're
close to the other entrance," he said. "And the
compass still shows us heading east. I think we
may be almost there."

They crossed the cavern and started
down the tunnel on the far side, but they hadn't
gone very much further when Pete noticed that
the space between the walls was widening, and
he saw what he thought was a glimmer of light.
They'd made it through!

"Yes!" Branko said. "I can see it. We
are almost there. I knew you'd do it!"

In the stillness, his voice sounded
strangely loud. So did Pete's. "And Jupiter's
question marks will get us back, if we need to
go that way!" he said.

"It is good to be with The Three Investigators," Branko said.

Just then, Pete heard what sounded like
someone sneezing in the tunnel ahead. It

probably wasn't a sneeze at all, but that was what it sounded like, and suddenly, Pete had a very uneasy feeling. After all, they were almost certainly not on Branko's family's property any more but on land belonging to the owner of Dragutin Wines.

In addition, as they entered what seemed to be the final passage leading to the outside, Pete had the strangest feeling that there had been someone in it just minutes before.

The cavern was big and high, but although there was a larger cave mouth on this side than on the other, and light was flooding into its front, it was still quite dark in the rear. Pete was torn between wanting to hurry forward to see if someone was hiding and hanging back while Jupiter moved deliberately, shining his flashlight over the walls around him.

The rock ceiling rose overhead and the walls stretched in a circling embrace. The floor was soft and sandy again – a relief after all that hard rock beneath his feet. Pete took a deep breath, but before the weight on his chest could start to lift, he noticed what smelled suspiciously like wood smoke. The hair on the back of his neck prickled. He'd been right. Someone *had* been here a little while before.

Pete shone his flashlight at the ground

near his feet and his heart leapt in his chest.

"Hey," he said. He didn't know why his voice came out in a harsh whisper, but he was suddenly afraid of being overheard. "Look at this!"

The charred remains of a campfire lay scattered in the sand. Beside it were some empty plastic water bottles.

Jupiter knelt and examined the evidence. "Clearly, someone has been here. And not long ago, either. The sand where the fire was built is still warm."

"Are you thinking what I'm thinking?" Bob said to Jupiter.

"I'm thinking that this campfire may be connected to the break-in at Dragutin last night," Jupiter said. "That this may be where the intruder spent the night."

Pete's flashlight had found footprints in the sand. "Over here!" he said.

The others crowded around. "Now I'm sorry I was in a hurry," Branko said. "We do not know if these are ours or someone else's."

But even before Jupiter pointed it out, Pete knew they were someone else's; those prints had been made by cowboy boots with a metal horseshoe cap on the heel.

"This is making me nervous," Pete said.

"Whoever was here is gone now,"Jupiter said. "We should take the time to see if he's left anything else behind."

Reluctantly Pete joined the others − all the while wishing Jupiter's curiosity wasn't so great. This was what came from a day that began with having to throw salt over his shoulder, he thought.

He was shining his light on the walls when Bob called out. "There's another passage over here! It's so dark at the back that we missed it. And what do you make of this?" Bob asked. His flashlight illuminated a black metal C-ring attached by bolts at the bottom of the cave wall.

"That's very interesting," Jupiter said as he knelt to investigate. "It's slightly worn on the outer side, so something like a rope has been threaded through it."

He shone his flashlight down the passage and its circle of light picked out three other metal C-rings. "We should follow this line of rings," Jupiter suggested.

Pete was not at all sure they should follow it; in fact, he thought they were going in the wrong direction entirely − away from the exit. If whoever had been in the cave came back, they'd be trapped, he thought. Or maybe the person he'd heard sneezing had hidden himself in this tunnel somewhere!

"Just as I suspected," Jupiter said. "All the rings show the same wear."

With Jupe in the lead, the four of them walked forward. Pete shone his light down the passage and was relieved to see a solid wall confronting them about forty feet away.

"This doesn't go anywhere. It's a dead end. Let's go back," he said.

But then he heard a thin scratching noise which seemed to be coming from above. He raised the beam of his flashlight until it met the ceiling.

"Watch out!" Jupiter yelled. Something swooped in the air above him – a falling of wings.

"A bat," Branko yelled and dove for the ground.

Pete was tempted to follow him. All the old stories about bloodsucking bats came swirling back into his head, and it took an effort of will to remember what he'd just learned.

"Where did that bat come from?" Bob asked, nervously.

"Up near the ceiling," Pete said.

They all turned their flashlights up there and saw what looked like ten or twenty little bundles of twigs wrapped round with leather.

"They must have sticky feet!" Branko said.

"They have little claws," Pete said. "They grasp onto something and their weight locks their claws in place." Pete thought about nightfall, when they would disattach from the rock and fly in a great rush out of the cavern's mouth.

"Since you're our animal expert," Bob said, "what kind of bats are those?"

"I think they're brown bats," Pete said. "But I don't know if they're little brown bats or big brown bats."

Bob laughed, a little nervously.

"No," Jupiter said. "Pete's right. Two entirely different species. I think those are actually little brown bats – *Myotis lucifugus*. Each one can eat over six hundred mosquitoes an hour. They're a great boon to farmers, and to all of us."

Somehow, finding the bats had made Pete feel less nervous. In fact, he was hardly nervous at all now. You weren't likely to find large numbers of bad guys hanging out where bats were roosting.

Jupiter had reached the end of the tunnel and Pete was close behind him as Jupiter shone his flashlight over the rock formation that closed the tunnel off. Pete was looking up at its corner when he saw a small black form squeeze its way through a tiny crack, then unfurl its wings and fly.

"Yikes!" Pete said. "That's weird! Did you see what I saw? It looked like that last bat was climbing out of another cavern!"

"But there couldn't be another cavern. Not here. This is solid rock," said Bob. "The bat must have just been tucked tightly in the corner."

"Maybe," said Pete doubtfully. "But it didn't look that way." He walked forward to the sloping tunnel wall, and as he pointed his flashlight upwards, he put his hand out to the wall to steady himself. When he did, he would have sworn that the rock felt less than perfectly solid. Experimentally, he thumped it.

"Do you hear that?" he asked Jupiter. "It sounds a little hollow."

Jupiter thumped it too.

"It does sound hollow," he said. "It also feels smoother than I would have expected."

Now Branko and Bob were standing next to them and thumping, too, and as they all thumped together, Pete's heart started beating faster – not with fear, but with the slowly growing understanding that what they were thumping wasn't real stone.

It was Bob who finally came out with it. "This isn't rock at all. I think it must be fiberglass, made to look like rock."

"I agree, Records," Jupiter said.

"Wow!" Pete said. "A fake wall! What's behind it, do you think? A bat cave?"

"Well, there may be bats *in* it," said Bob, "but I doubt it could be called a bat cave. The bats have taken advantage of the space, but I imagine it was sealed off for some other reason."

"If someone had wanted to seal it off for good, wouldn't they have used concrete?" asked Branko. "If it's fiberglass, then maybe it's a kind of door."

"That's an excellent observation, Branko," Jupiter said. "A door that leads to a cavern someone wanted to conceal. Still, if it *is* a door, we don't know how it opens."

"I wish we did!" Pete said, suddenly feeling adventurous again. "I wish we were here with Indiana Jones!"

"Well, we're here with Jupiter Jones," said Branko, "and to me, that seems just as good."

In the light from the flashlights, Pete

could see that Jupiter was looking both pleased and embarrassed by the compliment. He took his Swiss Army knife out, opened it, and dropped to his knees. He ran his flashlight slowly and carefully along the place where the fake wall met the rocky ground – at the same time that he ran the blade of his knife along it.

In short order his knife caught on something. It turned out to be a very clever clip – and once he had turned it, he moved on to find three others on the bottom. There were also clips on the sides, and along the top, and in order to get to the top ones, Jupiter had to climb on Pete and Branko's shoulders.

When the clips were finally unfastened, the four of them worked in concert to inch the large gray piece of fiberglass away from where it had been fastened. At last they were able to set it aside and to shine their flashlights into the cavern that lay behind it.

The first thing the light caught was what looked like a couple of hundred bats hanging peacefully upside down in a corner. Disturbed from their sleep, they turned their red eyes toward the boys, and a few were so startled they launched themselves into the air, filling the cavern with their high-pitched squeaks and the flapping of their wings.

They swooshed and sailed, darting at the boys and then veering up to the ceiling again, but this time, Branko didn't dive to the ground. Instead, the boys turned off their flashlights until the bats had settled back onto their perches – though as he stood waiting to turn his on again, Pete was almost certain he had seen light bulbs in zinc cages suspended from the ceiling.

"O.K.," said Jupiter when the bats were finally silent. "Let's turn our flashlights on again."

When they did, Pete took in everything quickly. He saw that a master electrical switch on the wall was connected to the lighting network, that an array of ancient, corroded batteries seemed to have been their power source, and that several heavy wooden tables stood waiting to be used again.

"Holy moly!" Pete said in a whisper.

By then all four of them had trained their flashlights on a large piece of heavy machinery that stood in the exact center of the cavern. It was big and black and boxy, with slanted surfaces and small metal platforms loaded with gears and levers and cylindrical rollers. Beside it was a pile of what looked like heavy electrical cables.

"What *is* that?" Pete asked.

"An offset printing press," Jupiter said. "Now we know what those rings in the wall were for. When the press was working, the electrical cables were plugged into it, then threaded through those C-rings in the tunnel. My guess is that there's a generator somewhere outside the cave's mouth. But I bet the engraving plates are stored somewhere in this cavern."

The engraving plates? Pete thought. *What* engraving plates? Then he gulped and almost shivered. Without even trying, they'd discovered the secret workshop of André Laurent, the ruthless, murdering French-Canadian counterfeiter!

"Come on!" Pete said. "Let's get out of here!"

7

Further Discoveries

It was ten minutes later, and Bob was still stunned by what they'd discovered. The previous morning his father had told him the stark details of a true-crime story that had happened twenty-five years before, and now that story had come to vivid life.

The murdering counterfeiter, who had fled Massachusetts and wound up in Jackson, had brought his expertise with him and had used it in this very cave. Had he worked alone? That seemed unlikely, when you considered how difficult it would have been to get the tables and press, the supplies and equipment into place.

Once the bats had settled back to sleep, Jupiter and Bob had explained to Branko what they'd stumbled on, then methodically searched the chamber and found a large brown suitcase and a smaller black one tucked under one of the wooden tables.

Now Branko and Pete were lifting them out and placing them on the tabletop. Bob watched as Jupiter opened the large one, then took out several stacks of paper. The paper was a creamy white, but also a little faded. The edges were crisply cut and the stack was exactly the size of paper money.

"Was he going to print on this?" Branko asked Jupiter.

"Counterfeiters are usually caught because the paper isn't right," Jupiter said. "Real greenbacks are printed on special cotton-rag paper, so expert counterfeiters like André Laurent sometimes get authentic paper by buying bundles of one-dollar bills, then bleaching all the dye out. That seems to be what has been done in the present instance.

"Quite wonderfully," he added, lifting up a single piece of paper and feeling it. He handed the paper around. Bob fingered it; it was thicker and heavier than most paper and felt substantial in his hand.

"What about this box?" asked Pete as he tried to flip the latches.

To everyone's surprise, the latches snapped open and when Jupiter raised the lid and shone his flashlight inside, it illuminated a number of engraved metal plates. From his backpack, Jupiter pulled the firm's magnifying glass, tucked into a leather pouch.

"You think of everything!" Pete said.

"One must be ready for all eventualities," Jupiter said. "Although, as we are discovering, life is full of surprises."

He adjusted his headlamp so that the line shone in the right direction and began examining one of the engraved plates, then another. Bending over them, with the others redirecting their lights to reduce the reflection, Jupiter looked to Bob a bit like a scientist hunched over a microscope.

"Just as I suspected," Jupiter said. "Each one of these plates is different. But if each engraving is printed, one on top of another, you'd get – "

"Lots and lots of hundred dollar bills!" Pete exclaimed.

"Impressive ones," said Jupiter. "Look at the circular lines around the portrait of Benjamin Franklin, Bob."

He passed the plate and the magnifying glass to Bob. Around Franklin's face a series of concentric lines, each perfectly spaced, gave depth and texture to the image.

Suddenly Bob felt strangely uneasy.

"I think we should take this stuff and go," he said.

"I agree," said Jupiter. "But let's be sure we haven't missed anything. We don't know when we'll be getting back."

"Hopefully never," Pete said. "Or at least not until we know where that Laurent guy is. Bob, didn't you say he got away before they could put him in jail?"

"That's what the article said," Bob told them. "He jumped bail."

"So he's on the loose," Pete said, nervously.

"I wouldn't be worried," Jupiter said. "We are clearly the first people in this room in many years. As for the man who lit the campfire, he's long gone."

He shone his flashlight into every corner, raking the walls and ceiling with its beam. He pointed out that the corroded batteries had been used to light the lights, and wondered if the generator would also be corroded. Finally he said, "All right. Let's go. I want to put the false wall back in place. Bob, you take the case with the paper, and Pete, you take the case with the engraving plates."

It took a bit of doing, but, together, the four of them were able to push the fake rock back into position and get its clips to click into place. In the cavern, they looked around one last time for further evidence about the identity of the man who had made such distinctive marks with his cowboy boots, and when they didn't find any, they headed for the cavern entrance.

They came out into a pleasant dappled light where some comfortable-looking flat rocks seemed almost to be waiting for them. When he saw them, Pete said, "I hate to mention it, but – "

"Let me guess," Bob said. "You're hungry."

"I can't believe it," Pete said, "but it's true.

"Suspense and excitement can either stimulate hunger or kill it," said Jupiter. "In Pete's case, it's almost always the first. But before we eat, I want to look for the generator."

"Oh, Jupe, let's eat first," Pete said. "I bet Branko's hungry, too."

"I am," Branko admitted.

"Well, you're our host," said Jupiter.

They each pulled whatever part of lunch they were carrying out of their backpacks and placed sandwiches, fruit, and bottled water on the stone. Bob found he was thirsty as well as hungry, and he drained his bottle of water in no time.

Meanwhile, Pete went about inspecting the sandwiches. There were three each of cheese and tomato, peanut butter and jelly, and egg salad, and in the end – not surprisingly – Pete ended up with the extra one.

After they had finished, Jupiter suggested that Bob put the case with the engraving plates into his backpack.

"The man who made those plates is a consummate professional – good enough, I'd say, to work at the Bureau of Engraving and Printing. It's amazing he was ever caught at all," Jupiter said.

"You said the Secret Service was after him?" Pete asked Bob.

"Yes," Bob said. "It turns out that the Secret Service was created at the end of the Civil War to investigate counterfeit greenbacks. If you can believe it, a third of the bills in circulation at the time were fake!"

"A country's economy depends on people believing that its bills are real," Jupiter said. "Fake money causes inflation and destabilizes the government. During World War II, the Germans counterfeited British pounds, hoping to create inflation. And our own CIA dropped huge amounts of fake currency from helicopters over Vietnam during the Vietnam war. Money has always been a useful weapon during war. Of course, a counterfeiter like André Laurent wouldn't care about any of that. He'd just want a way to launder his money."

"Those bills look pretty clean to me!" Pete said.

Branko thought that was very funny.

"All right," Jupiter said, "let's start looking. If there's still a generator around, it won't be far from the mouth of the cave."

As Jupiter shaded his eyes and scanned the area around the cave's mouth, Bob climbed a slight rise to the right where a tangle of mesquite and manzanita grew among boulders, in front of a rock protrusion. If he hadn't known what he was looking for, he would never have spotted it from a distance. But the moment he saw it, he knew he was looking at another manufactured stone – even though the manzanita and mesquite had grown up around the rock-like cover in the intervening years.

What surprised him was that the ground around the rock seemed disturbed – and in it were the same distinctive boot prints they had found in the cavern.

Bob called out, "Look at this!" and Jupiter climbed up to join him.

"Deductive reasoning suggested the presence of a hidden generator," Jupiter said.

"But we had to actually find it to discover that our friend from the cavern had gotten here before us."

When Pete and Branko also arrived, Jupiter got out his Swiss Army knife and repeated the process of disattaching the manufactured stone from its clips. Under it the generator had been bolted to a solid rock base, nestled into a natural formation that looked as if it had been designed to hold it. But it had also been covered with a tarp that had to be removed before they could be sure the generator was there.

Pete whistled. "Wow, here it is! And look at this!"

He lifted the edge of another tarp behind the generator and revealed a small stepladder and three metal propane tanks about two feet tall and a foot in diameter. There were also a few white pieces of paper that, upon examination, proved to be bleached dollar bills.

"I wonder why *those* are here," Bob said. "They can't have been lying on the concrete for twenty-five years without rotting, can they?"

"I don't think so," Jupiter said. "Perhaps the man who lit the campfire left them — or dropped them accidentally."

"But why would he do that?" asked

Branko.

"I don't know," Jupiter admitted. "I have no idea. But I assume that the stepladder was stored here so that the counterfeiters wouldn't need to sit on anyone's shoulders in order to reach the upper clips in the interior false wall. And these propane tanks are small enough to carry in a backpack. The operation seems to have been very clever."

Pete lifted one of the tanks and squinted in the bright light, making out the lettering on a paper label. "It holds eight gallons when it's full, and weighs thirty-three pounds. This label says it was last filled in 1995."

"The year André Laurent disappeared," Bob said.

When Jupiter suggested they do a further search of the area before they left, Bob said, "I bet I could find out more on my laptop in an hour than we could find out here in the next three days."

"No doubt you're right," Jupiter said. "We've found the physical evidence. Now we need to put it into context. We need background and history. We also need to decide how best to return. Through the cave? Or around?"

"I've had enough cave for today," Pete

said. "Let's stay outside."

"Besides," Bob said, "won't it be much quicker?"

"Yes, it will," Jupiter said. "But we should check with Branko. Will Mr. Ivan think we're trespassing on his land?"

"I do not think so," Branko said. "I do not know him, but most people around here are very forgiving. I also think he will have other things on his mind after the break-in."

"Which reminds me," Jupiter said. "I think it would be a good idea if we don't mention our discoveries to anyone – at least not yet. After what Branko's father said this morning at breakfast, the odds are good that Mr. Ivan would notify the police, and they would cordon off the cave and appropriate the evidence. I'd like to keep it private a bit longer."

They all agreed with this. After they bolted the cover back over the generator and tanks, Jupiter used the compass to orient them, and they took off at a good pace, hiking west-southwest. It took very little time before they reached the wire fence that marked the property line. Pete cupped his hands and one by one he hoisted Bob and the others over. And then he jumped over himself.

"Very good!" Branko said. "You are a

track and field star!"

"Just a soccer player," Pete said. "Do they have soccer in Serbia?"

"Of course!" said Branko. "But they call it football there."

"Just like they do in Italy," Pete said.

Back at the vineyard, they checked in with Branko's parents — to let them know they'd gotten back and to tell them they'd be spending the rest of the afternoon at the grape pickers' shed.

"Remember," Mr. Petrovic said. "The Pelletiers will be here later."

As they walked down the lane, Pete asked, "How many Pelletiers are there? Your father makes it sound like they're coming in a bus."

Branko laughed. "The Pelletier father is John," he said, "the mother is Emma, and their children are Lucas — the boy — and Harper — the girl. They are eleven — the age of Zivko."

"They are *both* eleven?" asked Jupiter.

"Twins," Branko answered.

"Twins!" Pete said. "Can you tell them apart?"

"If they're a boy and a girl," Jupiter said, "then I expect you can tell them apart quite easily. Boys and girls are always fraternal twins, not identical twins."

"That is correct," Branko said. "They are just like a brother and a sister but they were born at the same time."

"You said John Pelletier is a management consultant?" Jupiter asked.

"That is also correct," Branko said. "Three years ago, Mr. Cooper, who used to own Cornucopia, hired Mr. Pelletier to make things run better here."

"Did it work?" Jupiter asked.

"Very much," Branko said. "Papa says everything is easier now, and we are making more wine and it is better. Also, Papa and Mr. Pelletier became good friends. When we visited on weekends from Sonoma to see Papa, we all got to meet the Pelletiers. I like them very much, and the twins are unusual kids. They both belong to a 4-H Club, and take the club's activities very seriously. Even though they *are* the same age as Zivko, they seem older."

"That sounds like Jupiter!" Pete said. "Except that Jupiter formed his *own* club! Not that it's a club any more, of course. What does a 4-H Club do, anyway?"

"Well, the twins raise goats," said Branko.

"Goats!" Pete yelped. "I hope one of them isn't called Pete!"

"Their names are Penny and Zoey now," Branko said, smiling. "But originally they were called Cookie and Bubbles. Harper named them when she was only eight."

Bob opened the door to the grape pickers' shed and they all strode in. It was cooler and dimmer inside. Jupiter said he was going to lie down in his bunk for a while because he had thinking to do – and sometimes that worked best when he was on his back.

Branko got out a deck of cards and he and Pete sat at a small table at the far end of the room and got silly.

"Come play with us!" Branko called out. "We will play Go Fish! and Slapjack and other games to make us laugh."

That actually sounded inviting, but Bob had work to do. He got his laptop from the small room and situated himself near the router that extended the house's Wi-Fi. Behind him, Pete and Branko were slapping the table and chortling. At one point when he looked over, they were both holding cards up to their foreheads.

Bob began by searching through his computer's history to pull up the articles he'd discovered the morning before. They confirmed that in the mid-1990s the F.B.I. had shown up in Jackson to arrest a French-Canadian man named André Laurent. The authorities had never found the offset printing press he had used to print his counterfeit money.

Bob saw he needed to look farther and wider in order to find out more about Laurent himself. He began by typing "André Laurent," "counterfeiting," "Amador County," and "1995" into the search box. It turned out these were good choices.

He quickly found a number of articles from newspapers both in the Bay Area and in southern California, some more detailed than others. Most were datelined 1995. Bob was happy to see that more and more major papers had managed to digitize their archives, and he even found an article from the Los Angeles *Sun*, his father's paper. Before Bob got too far into any of this, he decided it would be best if Jupiter joined him. He walked into the small room where Jupiter lay on his bunk, his eyes closed.

"Jupe?" he said quietly.

Jupiter's eyes opened. He smiled. "Hello, Bob."

"Were you falling asleep?"

"No," Jupiter said. "I was just pondering. One would like to think the best of one's forebears, but if the man who originally owned Dragutin Wines was, indeed, my grandfather, then we have to wonder if he knew about the counterfeiting operation on his land. Perhaps he was even actively involved in it."

"Oh, I doubt that," Bob said – though he had actually already thought the same thing. "Anyway, I'm sure there's an explanation," he added, hoping that there was. "Come out and see what I've been finding."

With Jupiter sitting beside him, Bob read the articles he had bookmarked. He also showed Jupe the obituary he had found for Spiridon Markovic; it said that the owner of Dragutin Wines in Jackson, California had died suddenly in March of 1995 from a heart attack at the age of 50. Funeral services had been held at St. Sava's Eastern Orthodox Church in Jackson. Interment had followed in the church's cemetery.

Bob also pointed out that Spiridon Markovic had died over a month before André Laurent had been arrested.

"See?" Bob said. "Chances are he knew nothing at all."

"It's too early to conclude that," Jupiter

said. "But I must say that information comes as a relief. Perhaps you could also show me the family tree you constructed three or four days ago."

Bob hadn't yet had a chance to show Jupiter this half-factual half-fictional construction, but now he got onto the genealogy website and showed Jupiter the light blue box containing a slightly darker blue male profile with the black words "Jupiter Jones" in a white band at the bottom.

Above this was another blue box which read Claudius Jones, and a peach-colored box with a female profile which read Aleksandrina Markovic. Bob clicked on the box, then clicked again where it read "Profile" and found the following life story:

"Aleksandrina Markovic was born on April 12, in Jackson, California, the daughter of Nadja and Spiridon. She had one son with Claudius Jones. She died as a young mother in Toronto, Ontario, Canada, at the age of 23."

Bob had never clicked on the second box before and was amazed at how real this simple computer-generated biography seemed. It made the situation real for Jupiter, too, Bob could see; in fact, Jupiter looked stunned as he heard the words "young mother."

"Of course," Bob said, "we still don't have any reasonable explanation as to why Xandra would have changed her name to Amanda Morris – and even more important, as to why the only Amanda Morris I could find who matches what you know about your mother seems to have died at the age of five."

"Actually, I *do* have a reasonable explanation for the second point," Jupiter said hesitantly. "And maybe even for the first one. But I'd like to get Pete and Branko over here before we go any further."

"Pete! Branko!" Bob called. "Jupe wants us to do this together."

When the four of them were gathered around the laptop, Bob did his best to explain the way he'd constructed the half-factual half-fictional family tree.

He showed the others that Xandra's mother had been a woman named Nadja Dimitrijevic, and that her father was Spiridon Markovic.

Since Xandra's mother's father – one of Jupiter's great-grandparents – had been a man named Dranko Dimitrijevic who'd been born in 1897 in what was now Serbia – though he'd emigrated to the United States after the First World War – Xandra had had Serbian bloodlines through both of her parents.

"That's strange," Branko said. "Dimitrijevic was the name of the leader of a secret military group that assassinated the king and queen of Serbia in 1903."

"The Black Hand," Jupiter said.

"Yes!" Branko said. "You know of this?"

"I only know that a lot of people think the Black Hand was responsible for starting World War I when they assassinated Archduke Franz Ferdinand of Austria-Hungary," Jupiter said.

Bob plugged 'Dimitrijevic' and 'Black Hand' into his search engine, and the name Dragutin Dimitrijevic popped up, along with an encyclopedia article.

"Dragutin?" Pete exclaimed.

"Yes, that's right," said Branko. "His first name was Dragutin. I'd forgotten that."

Bob and the others stared at him in amazement.

"What?" Branko said. "Dragutin is a very common Serbian name. It just means 'precious.' Dimitrijevic is rarer."

"In any case," Jupiter said, "from what I can see — as well as from what Bob told me about his research — it was Xandra's father Spiridon who named Dragutin Wines. Since

Xandra's father got married ten years after he bought the vineyard, and Xandra's mother was the one descended from Dranko, he's unlikely to have named it for an ancestor of the wife he didn't yet have. Not that Dragutin Dimitrijevic could have been her ancestor, anyway. This article says he had no children and was executed in 1917 by a firing squad."

"Yikes!" Pete said. "That makes my head ache! Not the firing squad but the ancestor of the wife he didn't have yet!"

"Xandra's father Spiridon was born in a displaced persons camp in Yugoslavia in 1945," Bob told the others. "His parents came to America in 1947, when he was two."

"The day we met in Sonoma you said you knew nothing about your mother's family," Branko said. "They were political refugees?"

"Unfortunately, just because Bob created a file labeled Jupiter Jones and linked it to a box labeled Aleksandrina Markovic, that doesn't mean she was actually my mother," Jupiter said. "At this point, it's all conjecture. But I think we can trust Bob to have accurately discovered that Xandra Markovic's father's parents came to America seeking asylum – just as Bob's mother's parents did."

"Except that in *their* case, they were

coming from China," Bob clarified for Branko, who looked a bit confused.

"Anyway," Bob added, this time to Jupiter. "What's your reasonable explanation? Why might Xandra Markovic have changed her name to Amanda Morris? And what does it mean that the only Amanda Morris I could find who matched what I knew about your mother seems to have died at the age of five?"

"Before I tell you, let's do one more search for articles about André Laurent," Jupiter said.

Bob again typed "André Laurent," "counterfeiting," "Amador County," and "1995" into the search box. This time, he added "money laundering" and "extortion" and a detailed article originally published in the Auburn *Journal* suddenly popped up.

Bob read it quickly while the others waited. The article confirmed what they already knew, but added the information that a loan officer at a local Jackson bank had been arrested along with the counterfeiter.

"The loan officer's name was Mihailo Ivanisevic," Bob reported.

Jupiter's face went still. He walked to the wall and came back with one of the photographs he'd examined the day before.

"Here he is," Jupiter said, holding the photograph in front of him. "Mihailo Ivanisevic is the man who lent Spiridon Markovic the money to expand his business. What was he charged with?"

"Money laundering," Bob said, reading quickly. "Also fraud and conspiracy and extortion. He was supposedly an accomplice of André Laurent. They arrested him on the testimony of a witness. But he claimed that André Laurent had been extorting *him* – that he'd threatened to burn down St. Sava's if Ivanisevic didn't help him launder his counterfeit money through his bank. The jury believed him, and acquitted him."

"Burn down St. Sava's!" Branko exclaimed, shocked. "No wonder he cooperated. The church is the center of the Serbian community in Jackson – and although I am not a believer myself, at least I believe you shouldn't burn down churches!"

"Who was the witness?" Pete asked.

"It doesn't give her name," Bob said, "but she was the widow of a local vineyard owner. She testified that Mihailo Ivanisevic and André Laurent had coerced her husband into helping them with their scheme. Her husband had owed the bank money and Ivanisevic told him that if he didn't help them with their counterfeiting scheme, the bank was going to foreclose on the loan. He'd have lost everything."

"Wow!" said Pete. "The vineyard almost *had* to be Dragutin! But why don't they name the witness?"

"I think I can answer that," Jupiter said, quite grimly.

8

Penny and Zoey Make An Important Find

It was half an hour later, and Jupiter had finally finished explaining his current theory to Pete, Bob, and Branko. He'd actually found himself getting more excited the longer he'd talked; only then had he fully realized everything he'd come to understand.

Of course, even before Bob had found the article in the Auburn *Journal*, Jupiter had thought he knew why Aleksandrina Markovic might have changed her name – and why the only Amanda Morris Bob could find, with the proper birthday, had died at the young age of five.

After all, Jupiter had long known that one of the best ways to erase your old identity and create a new one was to get your hands on detailed information about a baby who'd been born on the same approximate date that you had, but who had died quite young.

But he hadn't known until Bob found the article in the Auburn *Journal* why Xandra Markovic might have wanted to disappear.

Now he *did* know. Or at least he thought he did. Of course, it hadn't been Xandra herself who had wanted to disappear. She had only been twelve years old at the time. No, it must have been her mother, Nadja, who'd felt that she and her daughter needed to disappear together.

To Jupiter's mind, the fact that the counterfeiting equipment had been hidden in the cave at the the back of the Dragutin Vineyard made it almost certain that the unnamed widow referred to in the article had been Xandra's mother, Nadja.

In addition, the way the article had been written – no mention of the name of either the witness or the vineyard – strongly suggested that Nadja had been put into the federal witness protection program in exchange for testifying against André Laurent and Mihailo Ivanisevic.

If that was true, it was also almost certain that Aleksandrina Markovic had been Jupiter's mother, and that the Jones Family Tree which Bob had created on the genealogy website was a lot more factual than fictional. Granted, it still had large gaps in its branches, and Jupiter wished he knew whether either of Xandra's parents had had brothers or sisters.

As it was, the family tree grew *up* more than it grew *out*.

Still, unsettled as he was by the discoveries of the afternoon, Jupiter knew he had to put them out of his mind for the time being. The Petrovics had been kind to invite The Three Investigators up to Jackson, and he wanted to be an appreciative guest. It would be difficult – once he started thinking about something, his obsessive nature took over – but he would, at the least, need to *pretend* that his mind was solely on the cookout.

Branko had gone to the main house to check on everything, saying he'd be back to get his friends at 5. Jupiter, Pete, and Bob would each have time to take a shower and change into their best clothes. As always, it was important that they make a good impression.

As Jupiter stood with the hot water pounding on his shoulders, he thought again about what he had learned. The unnamed widow who had testified against Mihailo Ivanisevic had to have been Xandra Markovic's mother – a woman who was almost certainly Jupiter's grandmother. Presumably when she and her daughter had been put into the witness protection program, she had had to sell the vineyard.

As for the offset press, the engraving plates, and the bleached dollar bills, he thought that The Three Investigators had learned all they could about them. What still needed to be discovered about the present situation was who had been camping in the cave, and whether or not that person had, indeed, been the person who had broken into the wine cave at Dragutin.

Jupiter had dried himself off and dressed and was still thinking about these questions when Branko reappeared.

"Come, my friends," he said. "It is time now for the picnic." He went to Pete, put his hand on his shoulder, and looked at him with amusement. "I am sorry to tell you, but my mother has been cooking all day."

"Oh, no," Pete said.

"You will like it," Branko said. "You must take it easy, however."

Then he turned to Jupiter. "In your honor, tonight we have a Serbian cookout. Tomorrow, in honor of the United States of America, we have an American cookout."

"So what's on the menu tonight?" Bob asked.

"Oh, many things," Branko said. "We

will start with salad. We will have tomatoes and onions and cucumbers from my father's garden, with oil and vinegar. I think my mother made gibanjica, which is a cheese pie, very delicious. Then stuffed cabbage. Kebabs on the fire. And chevaps. Very tasty."

"Is there anything else we need to know about this evening?" Bob said, smiling.

"I do not think so," Branko said. "I have told you about the Pelletiers. We will probably sit with the grown-ups and the four children will play with one another."

Jupiter was a bit uneasy. Because of all that was on his mind, he was feeling less than gregarious, and his preferred style of conversation was one-on-one. With so many new people to meet, it might prove difficult.

They were warmly welcomed back at the house by Branko's parents. In spite of how busy they were – working in the kitchen, lighting the fire in the outdoor fireplace – they were eager to hear how Jupiter and the others had enjoyed the cave. Jupiter realized they were just being polite, because Branko had probably told them all about it earlier. Besides, without the climax to the story, there wasn't much to tell.

Everyone was in high spirits, Zivko and

Milena giggling and running from place to place, when the Pelletiers arrived in a big yellow van with lots of seats and lots of windows. Everyone went out to meet them.

"Welcome to Cornucopia, my friends," Mr. Petrovic said as the family got out of the van.

John Pelletier was tallish, with the broad shoulders of a boxer. He had blondish hair, and wore a large straw gardening hat to keep the sun off his face, khaki pants, and a blue button-down shirt with the cuffs rolled up. He had a quiet reserve, and Jupiter could see that he might not be easy to talk to. But when Mr. Petrovic approached him, the two men embraced like brothers.

Emma Pelletier had short brown hair and a quick vivacious smile. She wore a pretty flower-bedecked sundress.

"Jelena," she said as she kissed Mrs. Petrovic on each cheek. She handed her a bright bouquet.

Luke and Harper favored their father, and although they were certainly not identical, they looked remarkably alike, Jupiter thought. They had the same eyes, the same noses, the same chins. No one could have ever doubted they were brother and sister.

They also shared an intensity of gaze and a stillness of body that made them seem – at least at first meeting – the diametric opposites to their friends Zivko and Milena. Branko had been right, Jupiter thought.

However, Luke was taller and seemed to be accustomed to taking the lead in social situations. He introduced himself and his sister while she stood gravely beside him, fingering a leather pouch she wore over her shoulder on a long thin strap.

When Bob smiled and remarked, "We hear you're in a 4-H Club," it was Luke who said, "Yes, we raise goats."

At that point, Zivko showed up and the two boys laughed and fist-bumped and soon were running off around the back of the house, followed by a barking Zeus. Harper seemed glad when Pete bent down and said, "Your goats are named Cookie and Bubbles?"

"They were," Harper answered. "And we still use those names sometimes. But we've changed their names in our records. They're now Penny and Zoey. Penny is black, and Zoey is brown and white."

"They're Nubians," said Milena, clearly trying to be helpful. "With big soft ears."

"Come, everyone," Mr. Petrovic said.

"We will go to the back where the tables are set."

There, the smell of cooking was starting to fill the air. Mrs. Petrovic and Mrs. Pelletier had already carried baskets of bread, and platters of cheese and tomatoes and cucumber salad to the table, which had been set with vases of nasturtiums, stoneware plates, and bright orange napkins.

By the time Jupiter arrived, Mr. Petrovic was pouring wine into small tumblers. He passed one to Mr. Pelletier and another to Mrs. Pelletier. Then he called the boys over. "It will not hurt, I think," he said, "if you taste a little of Cornucopia wine. Besides, I wish to make a toast to you."

Jupiter, Pete, Bob, and Branko all were given a glass. Jupiter swirled the liquid as he held it. It was good and dark, more black than red, and it left a film on the side.

Mr. Petrovic raised his glass.

"To friends, old and new," he said.

He nodded cordially to the Pelletiers, and then turned to Jupiter, Pete, and Bob. "We are glad to have you here in Jackson," he said, "to celebrate The Three Investigators. And we are glad to celebrate our Serbian friend, Jupiter Jones."

Jupiter felt a bit embarrassed. He did not relish this kind of public attention and scrutiny. Everyone raised their glass and said, "To friends." Jupiter took a sip of the wine. It was heady and strong and tasted of cinnamon.

Mr. Pelletier came over to Jupiter. "So you are Serbian?" he asked.

"I have some Serbian blood, I think," Jupiter said. "My mother was Serbian, from what I can tell."

"I also have some Serbian family, though my father was French-Canadian," Mr. Pelletier said. "Miro – " He nodded in the direction of Mr. Petrovic – "tells me you and your friends are detectives."

"That's correct," Jupiter said. "We investigate anything. Well, anything that comes to our attention," he clarified. He produced a Three Investigators' card from his pocket and handed it to Mr. Pelletier. The card said, as it always had:

THE THREE INVESTIGATORS
"We Investigate Anything"
???

First Investigator – Jupiter Jones
Second Investigator – Pete Crenshaw
Records and Research – Bob Andrews

At the bottom was the website address of their firm, the number of the landline in Headquarters, and the number of Bob's cellphone.

John Pelletier examined the card carefully, then looked back at Jupiter. "The question marks?" he asked.

"That is our trademark," Jupiter said. "The universal symbol of mystery."

"So much of life is mystery," Mr. Pelletier said. "I look at my children, who have my hair and my eyes, and I wonder where in them is their grandmother – who is much darker. But then I see that they share her intensity and focus."

He looked at Harper who was now talking intently with Milena and then at Luke who ran by, laughing, with Zivko.

"Luke is the more easy-going of the two," he said, "at least on the surface."

Jupiter looked at the children and for a fleeting moment had a sense of Mr. Pelletier's paternal pride. He could tell from the expression on his face and the tone of his voice how close he was to the twins. He found himself drawn to the man.

"Yes," Jupiter said. "Genetic inheritance is unassailable but sometimes not immediately visible."

Mr. Pelletier's expression did not change as he looked down at Jupiter. "Perhaps you and your friends could investigate something for me," he said.

"We'd be happy to," said Jupiter. "What would you like us to look into?"

"For the time being, that will have to remain a mystery," Mr. Pelletier said, smiling. "I can't go into details right now, and we ought to enjoy ourselves, since Miro and Jelena have gone to so much trouble on our behalf. But why don't you and your friends come to my house tomorrow morning? Say about ten o'clock? We can talk about it then. Unless you plan to attend church with the Petrovics."

"We're not churchgoers, and Branko isn't, either," said Jupiter. "But our car won't be back in Jackson until tomorrow afternoon. We only have our bicycles. Do you live nearby?"

"We live right across from Dragutin Wines," said Mr. Pelletier. "My mother and father bought the property a long time ago, and when my father died fifteen years ago, my mother asked my family to come and live with her. From here, it's an easy bike ride – a bit uphill for part of the way, but nothing too hard. You'll know you've gone too far if you get to a place with a bull."

"A bull?" asked Jupiter, raising his eyebrows.

"Our neighbors to the east raise grass-fed beef," Mr. Pelletier explained.

"I'll confer with my friends and unless they have plans I don't know about, Pete, Bob, Branko, and I will plan on biking to your house tomorrow morning," Jupiter said.

"I'll look forward to it," Mr. Pelletier said. He reached out to shake Jupiter's hand, and Jupiter took it and shook it firmly. Though he knew he had never met Mr. Pelletier before, there was something familiar about him. He could not think who the man reminded him of.

Jupiter's mind was whirring. He thought he had come to Jackson to find out more about his family, but suddenly there were more mysteries and investigations than he could count. What did Mr. Pelletier want The Three Investigators to investigate? And who had lit the fire in the cave? Who had broken into the Dragutin wine cave, and why?

Jupiter knew he would have to sort these things out later. Keeping in mind his decision to be a good guest, he went over to Harper who was standing talking with Bob and Pete, a serious expression on her face. When Jupiter arrived, Pete was asking, "Are goats a lot of work?"

Harper looked at him earnestly. "I think of work as something you have to do that you don't really want to do."

"That's an interesting distinction," Jupiter said.

Harper glanced at him and added, in an explanatory tone, "They're a lot of responsibility. Luke and I have to feed and water them twice a day and keep their pen clean. And since they're dairy goats we need to milk them, and sell the milk at the farmer's market."

Jupiter was impressed by her matter-of-fact tone. She seemed very mature for an eleven-year-old – though no more mature than *he* had been when he was eleven, he thought.

"You said earlier that you kept records. Is that what you have in your shoulder pouch?" he asked.

Harper looked down at the pouch and then up at Jupiter. "Oh, no," she said. "All my records are on my computer. I just have a pad in there to keep track of what I see – especially when I'm around the goats. I write down observations and questions so I can do research later."

Jupiter could see that Harper had a natural curiosity about the world and an interest in finding out why it worked the way it did. This was something they had in common.

"Goats are very inquisitive," Harper added, "and they can get into all sorts of trouble. They'll eat just about anything if you let them. Both Penny and Zoey ate a bunch of paper yesterday."

"Paper?" Bob said. "Where did they get paper?"

"They like to walk around the wire fence at the edge of our property," Harper said, "and sometimes they stick their heads through and eat what's on the other side. Yesterday they found a bunch of paper, and they would probably have eaten all of it if our neighbor's bull hadn't scared them away."

"There's a bull?" Pete asked.

"The neighbors run a grass-fed beef operation," Jupiter explained to his friends. "The Pelletiers live across from Dragutin Wines — just below what must be a sort of mini-ranch. Mr. Pelletier has just asked us to investigate something for him, so unless Branko has other plans, we'll be seeing both places tomorrow."

"I don't plan on seeing that bull, if I can help it," said Pete emphatically.

"Actually, he's usually pretty gentle," Harper said. "But he doesn't like strange people, and he gets irritated at the sight of goats. When he saw Penny and Zoey sticking their heads through the fence, he charged them – which turned out to be a good thing, because they stopped eating the paper."

"Was it newspaper?" Jupiter asked. "Were you worried about them ingesting the ink?"

"Oh, no," Harper said. "Newspaper is all wood pulp, but this was much thicker and heavier. My father said he thought it was cotton bond. It was white, anyway. And since it was cellulose, the goats could digest it pretty well. They have bacteria in their rumens — that's the first chamber of their stomachs — which break down the cellulose and let them digest it. Anyway, luckily, it was cut into little pieces. There was a leather carrying bag next to it. My father recovered the uneaten paper and the bag so that Penny and Zoey couldn't get at any of it again."

Jupiter found he was suddenly paying closer attention. Lots of little pieces of white paper that Mr. Pelletier thought might be cotton bond sounded a lot like a bunch of one-dollar bills that had been bleached of all ink, he thought.

"When did this happen?" he asked. "And how big were the little pieces?"

"If you want to see the paper, I have a piece of it in my notebook. I put it there yesterday morning," Harper answered.

Jupiter felt a jolt of excitement.

"I'd be very interested to see it," he said.

Harper opened the flap of her small leather bag, then drew out a black notebook with a rubber band holding it closed. She took off the rubber band, opened the notebook, and drew out from the space between the back cover and the final page a small white folded wad.

"If Penny and Zoey had gotten sick, I was going to give the paper to the vet to have it chemically analyzed," she said, unfolding it carefully, then proffering the result.

So much for putting the discoveries of the afternoon out of his mind, Jupiter thought, as Pete and Bob both exclaimed "Yikes!" He looked at them in warning, then took the paper, examined it, and handed it back.

"I wish all the people we deal with in our investigations were as careful in their observations and record-keeping as you are," he said.

Harper smiled in apparent agreement as

she refolded the paper, then tucked it back into her notebook.

"I like being careful about things," she said.

Just then, Zivko and Milena and Luke appeared to say that their mothers wanted some help. Harper walked off with them, while Bob and Pete looked at Jupiter with a combination of excitement and alarm.

"Are you thinking what I'm thinking?" Pete asked.

"If you're thinking that the man who took refuge in the cave last night was almost certainly the man who dropped the satchel of paper in the bull's field, then yes," Jupiter said. "I surmise that the bleached bills we found next to the propane tanks had fallen out of the carrying bag Harper described."

"I'm also thinking that the reason he dropped the bag was that he had to run for his life when he found himself in a pasture with an angry bull," Pete said.

"I'd say that's a good deduction," Jupiter said.

"If we went to look," Bob said, "maybe we'd find boot prints like the ones in the cave."

"We can do that tomorrow," Jupiter said, "when we visit Mr. Pelletier to find out what mystery he wants us to investigate."

"Is it about the counterfeiting, do you think?" Bob asked.

"It could be," Jupiter said, "or it could be something else entirely. We'll have to wait until tomorrow to find out."

The ringing of a bell stopped the conversation short.

"Come!" said Mr. Petrovic. "Let us all sit down! Kebabs and chevaps for everyone! And later we dance the kolo!"

Jupiter had to admit that he hoped not. He had a lot on his mind, and dancing the kolo was the last item on his list.

9

An Unexpected Visitor

The next morning, as Pete and the others were strolling back to the bunkhouse from the main house after eating breakfast, Pete was thinking about how funny Jupiter had looked the night before. After dinner and dessert, as the small twinkling lights the Petrovics had put in the trees overhead came on, everyone had joined hands in a circle and Mr. Petrovic had tried to teach the newcomers how to dance the Serbian national dance.

Pete and Bob had caught on fast — though they hadn't tried the intricate variations that Branko and his father dazzled them with. But even though the basic dance was easy, Jupiter couldn't seem to get the hang of it.

"I guess dancing the kolo isn't heritable," Bob had quipped.

As it turned out, Pete wasn't the only one remembering this event, because as the four of them kept walking toward the bunkhouse, Branko sidled up to Jupiter and did a little step to the right, followed by a hop and a step to the left. Pete and Bob burst out laughing.

"Go on," Pete said to Jupe. "Maybe you can do better today."

Though Jupiter was good-natured about the kidding, Pete could see he was a bit stung by it.

"I was thinking hard about other things last night," he reminded them. "I'm sure that next time I'll improve."

He put his hand on Branko's shoulder and Branko put his hand on Jupe's, and together they stepped and hopped to the right, then the left, then the right again, moving to invisible music.

"Bravo!" Branko said. "My Serbian brother!"

When they got back to the bunkhouse, Jupiter said, "We've got an hour before we have to leave for the Pelletiers, and I think we should use it to analyze these articles on the wall, in case there's something we've missed. We're looking for anything that might have a bearing on the counterfeiting or on Dragutin Wines."

Along with his friends, Pete got to work. He hadn't really looked at the framed articles before. Most were old and yellowed and diffi-cult to read − though there were lots of interesting facts about the vineyards of Amador County, the winemaking process, and the history of Jackson. He wondered who had chosen these particular clippings; it clearly had happened long before the Petrovics' time.

Pete was reading an article from years before about the number of new wineries in Amador County when Jupiter called out, "Listen to this. Remember when Mr. Petrovic said that Spiridon Markovic had money problems? It seems a number of local vineyards were encouraged to take out bank loans for improvements to their operations in the early 1990s, after interest rates briefly fell. But since they were variable loans, when interest rates rose again, payments to the bank quickly shot through the roof."

"What's a variable loan?" Pete asked.

"A loan where the amount of money you owe the bank changes when the interest rate changes," Jupiter said. "You borrow money at a certain interest rate and make payments based on that. But if the interest rate goes up, so does your payment. The article says that between 1992 and 1995, four separate vineyards had their loans foreclosed when interest rates rose again. The vineyard owners couldn't meet their payments, and they lost their businesses."

"Wow!" Pete said. "That doesn't seem fair at all."

Though Pete knew it wasn't very mature of him to be bored by this discussion, he was, anyway – though he continued to study the articles on the wall. When he found one that seemed at least mildly exciting, he lifted it off, went to the table, and read it, surrounded by the others.

"Look," he said. "In March 1992 someone set fire to St. Sava's. Just a small fire, in an anteroom. The fire department was there in no time; some anonymous caller dialed 911. The chief of the department said it was almost as if whoever set the fire also made the call so no real damage was done."

"But why would an arsonist do that?" Branko asked. "He had a change of heart?"

"He probably wanted to show what he could do if he wanted to," Jupiter said. "Remember the article Bob found yesterday? Ivanisevic, the loan officer, testified that André Laurent threatened to burn down St. Sava's if he didn't launder the counterfeit money. I think Laurent was demonstrating his intentions at a time when Ivanisevic was refusing to cooperate. A quite persuasive threat."

"Wow," Bob said. "That makes sense.

In 1992 Laurent must have been just starting to get his operation underway — three whole years before he and Ivanisevic were caught."

"Yes," Jupiter said. "And three whole years before Spiridon Marcovic died."

He paused. "You all thought it was funny that I had a hard time dancing the kolo last night. But I was just concluding that the man who broke into the Dragutin wine cave, left his boot prints in the sand, and uncovered the generator was André Laurent himself. My mind wasn't on dancing."

"So you *do* think he's back in town!" Pete said, suddenly realizing that this was exactly what he'd thought himself.

"Unfortunately, yes," said Jupiter. "Logically, there could only have been three men who knew the whereabouts of the generator — Spiridon Marcovic, Mihailo Ivanisevic, and André Laurent himself. One of them is dead; one of them is who knows where; and the third is the only one who would have wanted to get the generator operating again.

"I'd bet that when he discovered the generator didn't work, he abandoned his original plan to open up the cavern with the printing press — but grabbed the bag of paper just in case he had another chance to use it."

"Even if the generator didn't work, wouldn't he have wanted to get the engraving plates?" Bob asked.

"I don't know," Jupiter said. "He may have been planning to recover the engraving plates just at the moment we got to the cavern. If so, I'm glad we got there first."

"So you think he may still want those plates?" Pete said.

"I wouldn't be surprised," Jupiter said.

Pete's heart started pounding a little bit.

"Well, then, shouldn't we at least *hide* them?" he said. "I don't like the idea that they're right here in this bunkhouse where we go to sleep at night!"

"Are you suggesting that we ought to be worried, just because a guy who's committed murder, blackmail, forgery, counterfeiting, arson, and extortion may be after something we're holding?" Bob asked, grinning.

"You bet I am!" Pete said. "I think we should get those plates out of here now!"

"You may be right," Jupiter said. "But luckily, Laurent has no idea who we are and no idea where we're staying. And we don't have time to worry about it at the moment." He glanced at his watch.

"We're due at the Pelletiers' house at 10

o'clock," he said. "How long does it take to get there by bike, Branko?"

"About fifteen minutes," Branko said.

"Then we'd better go," Jupiter said.

As the four of them went outside, Pete thought that even if the plates *were* in the bunkhouse, at least the four of them weren't in there with them. And Laurent *didn't* know who they were or where they were staying. Jupiter was right about that.

Since Branko's family had already left for church at St. Sava's the four boys simply buckled on their bike helmets and took off, arriving at the Pelletiers' right on time. Being on time always made Pete happy.

The Pelletiers' house was white clapboard, with a green standing-seam metal roof and a wraparound porch. It gave the impression of being both large and cozy at once, and it seemed to Pete as though it had started out small and gotten bigger over the years. He wouldn't have been surprised if it was over a hundred years old, and it had an openness and optimism about it − a fresh-air feel − as though it were actually on the sea.

Set in the middle of a five-acre plot, it had some elevation and thus several lovely views, up into the mountains to the east and down toward several vineyards in the valley be-low. It was across the road from the lower part of Dragutin Wines, and when the boys got there, Mr. and Mrs. Pelletier and Luke and Harper were waiting for them on the front porch. Pete had liked Luke and Harper when he'd met them the night before, and he was glad to see them again. Luke picked up a tray with a pitcher of fresh goat's milk and four little glasses.

"We thought you might like some milk," Harper said, carefully setting one glass in the hands of each of the four boys. Pete guessed that, as a girl with a twin brother, Harper must feel more comfortable around boys than many girls her age did. Although Pete had never had goat's milk before, he found he liked it — though he could tell that Bob didn't. About Ju-piter, he had no idea.

"Welcome!" John Pelletier said. "But be-fore we retire to my study to discuss the mys-tery, Luke and Harper want to show you their goat operation. Now, don't tell them *everything* you know about goats," he added to Harper. "Save something for next time. And bring them back to the house when you're finished."

Pete, Branko, Bob, and Jupiter followed the twins off the porch and up a field above which Pete could see cattle grazing. That must be where André Laurent had been chased by an angry bull, he realized. Pete couldn't see any bull in evidence just now, but as they approached the end of the Pelletiers' field, two goats came running out to greet them.

One of them was jet black, and the other was a warm chocolate brown with blond ears. Both had rounded noses and their ears were luxurious, long, and floppy, hanging down below their chins. They looked to Pete both antic and exotic as they came and butted him, looking for food he might have hidden in his hands.

"This is Penny and this is Zoey," Harper said, patting first one and then the other. "Connor O'Malley says they're relentless."

Pete looked at her in astonishment.

"Connor O'Malley?" he exclaimed.

"He's our Four-H Club sponsor," Luke said.

"You mean Connor O'Malley from Auburn?" Pete said.

"Yes," Luke said, looking at Pete oddly. "Do you know him?"

"I sure do!" Pete said. "We all do − well, not Branko. The rest of us rescued a great horned owl with him. Give him our best wishes when you see him!"

"We're actually going to see him tomorrow night," Luke said. "He's coming to see how we're doing with the goats, and he always stays for dinner after he's checked on them."

Pete had really liked Connor O'Malley, and he hoped he'd get to see him on his visit to Jackson. However, he was aware that, at the moment, Jupiter was fully focused on the present case.

"Can you show us where you found the paper?" he asked Luke and Harper.

"Totally," said Luke.

Leaving the goats behind, he and Harper led the way to a sturdy wire fence, and as Bob, Jupiter, and Branko knelt next to it, looking for footprints in the dirt on the other side, Pete stared past it to a grassy field in which he saw what looked like a small square black house begin to move in the distance.

"Uh, guys, you might want to back off a little," he said.

"We can't seem to see any prints from cowboy boots," Bob said. "What are you staring at, Pete?"

"*That*," said Pete, pointing. The other three followed the direction of his finger, then stood up quickly, backed away from the fence, and watched as the bull approached at an angle – and at an enthusiastic canter.

"He's in a good mood today," Harper said. "We may even get to pet him."

Jupiter, Branko, and Bob weren't so sure and stepped back even further from the wire, but Pete stayed where he was. The bull stopped about ten feet away and then slowly came closer and closer until Pete could have reached out and touched him.

Instead, he held his hand out just far enough to feel the bull's hot breath on the palm of his hand. The bull's horns were sharp, and he was massive, but his dark eyes were mild and looked at Pete with something like amusement. Maybe the bull was a good judge of character and only harassed and chased bad guys like André Laurent, Pete thought.

Once the bull had moved down the field, Jupiter pointed to a water trough and spigot. "That would explain what André Laurent was doing in the field in the first place," he said. "Remember the empty water bottles next to the abandoned fire?"

"You mean he was trying to get some water when the bull surprised him?" Pete said.

"Presumably," Jupiter said. "I've been wondering what could have taken him into a field with a bull in the first place. The cave has no water, and he's been traveling light. He was probably simply thirsty and didn't see the bull until it was too late."

"Who's André Laurent?" asked Harper.

"What cave has no water?" asked Luke.

Jupiter looked at them as if he had forgotten they were there. Later, Pete thought of lots of ways he could have answered them without actually answering, but for some reason, he told them the truth.

"We think the man who dropped the bag with the paper your goats ate was actually staying in a cave on Dragutin land," Jupiter said. "He might be a man who lived in Jackson a long time ago, before you were born. If we're right, he isn't very honest and he may be pretty dangerous. We think he was chased by the bull when he was getting water."

"That would explain why he dropped the bag," Harper said. "Do you think he'll try and get it back? We gave it to my father. It's in the house now."

"Maybe you should go and see it," Luke said. "That's what he wants to talk to you about."

"Let's go, then," said Jupiter.

The six of them walked back down the field, while Pete wondered who Harper reminded him of. When they got to the shed, Harper and Luke said that they had to sterilize their milking equipment, so the boys continued on to the house without them. Mr. Pelletier was waiting for them on the porch again.

"Emma's gone down the road to check on one of our neighbors who wasn't feeling well," he said, "but I want you to come in and meet my mother."

The living room was spacious, with a bay window overlooking the yard, and as Pete and the others entered, a woman rose from a desk tucked into a corner. Pete couldn't tell how old she was, but she didn't seem old. Her gestures as she shook their hands were emphatic and she bristled with energy. Her hair was still dark, with streaks of gray, and cropped short – a no-nonsense cut that suggested she had more important things to worry about than her hair. Her eyes and smile were bright.

"This is my mother Dora," Mr. Pelletier said. "And please, call me John."

Dora greeted them with nods and hellos, then followed as her son herded the boys into his study, where everyone sat down.

"I might as well get right to it," John said. "I know from my experience with the twins that adults are constantly underrating the capacities of young people, and, as you will quickly come to understand, this is something I don't want to involve the police in at the moment."

From under his desk he pulled a worn leather satchel with two handles that came together when it was zipped. On its side, Pete could see two faded gold embossed letters – A.L. Was there a chill in the air suddenly? Pete looked at his friends as John Pelletier took out several piles of bleached paper.

Then, as the boys peered closer, he opened the satchel wide and showed them its rigid bottom. It didn't look like a false bottom, but John Pelletier retrieved a small assortment of papers from underneath it. He set the papers on the desk, then extracted a somewhat crumpled photograph which he handed to Jupiter to study.

"I told Jupiter my father was French-Canadian," he said, "and you'll notice that under the photo are the names of the students of the 1965 graduating class of St. John's Academy in Montreal. Robert Pelletier was my father, but until I discovered what was hidden in this satchel, I had no idea — none whatever — that he had gone to school with a man named

André Laurent. I was just a boy when Laurent was arrested, but my father never mentioned to either my mother or me that he had ever known him."

"What else was in the satchel?" Jupiter asked, handing the photograph to the others.

John lifted an index card and silently handed it to Jupiter, who shortly passed it on to the other boys. It was faded, but it had the name, phone number, and address of one Robert Pelletier written in a blunt strong hand, in ink. Pete saw that the address was the address of the house they were currently visiting.

"Also, there was this."

This time Pete found himself holding an article from the Boston *Globe* about the murder of Laurent's partner. It had a picture of the counterfeiter in which he looked hard and angry.

Last – but not least, in Pete's opinion – were five $100 bills.

Jupiter held the bills in his hand a long time before he passed them on. Then he said, "I appreciate your trust in us, Mr. Pelletier, and wish to reciprocate. For reasons I don't entirely understand, I feel sure I can entrust the two of you with the information I'm about to give you."

"Of course," John Pelletier said, and his mother nodded vigorously.

"As I'm sure you recollect," Jupiter said, "André Laurent jumped bail before he could go to trial. Where he's been for the past twenty-five years is a mystery, but logic suggests that he is now back in Jackson."

Pete watched as expressions of dismay settled on the Pelletiers' faces.

"I was afraid of that," John said.

"Pete, Bob, Branko, and I discovered his old lair behind a false rock wall in a cave that connects Cornucopia Wines with Dragutin Wines," Jupiter said. "We found the offset printing press he used, the engraving plates for printing $100 bills like the ones you discovered, and a suitcase of paper like the paper Penny and Zoey ate."

"Those $100 bills look like the real thing," Dora Pelletier said.

Jupiter nodded in agreement. "But more importantly, we also found the remains of a fire in that cave, and footprints both inside and outside the cave – near a hidden generator that powered the printing press and where I think Laurent had stowed that satchel many years ago. My guess is that he's the one who broke into the wine cave at Dragutin, looking for something else he left behind. But we don't yet understand why he waited so long to come back here."

"This is amazing," Dora Pelletier said. "It seems you've discovered more in a few days than law enforcement found out in a quarter century."

"Where do you think Laurent has been?" John Pelletier asked.

"That's a good question," Jupiter said. "It makes little sense that he stayed away so long — and equally little sense that he's come back now."

"A guy like him is a criminal," Pete said, "and criminals have a hard time staying out of jail. Maybe he's been locked up all these years for another crime and he's just been released."

"But if that's true," John Pelletier said, "surely there would be an article about it on the Internet. The authorities would have connected him to the earlier crimes. It would have been a big story."

"It would seem so," Jupiter agreed, "but the trail goes cold in 1995 when Laurent vanished after jumping bail."

"Maybe he used a false name. Maybe he had a fake ID," Pete suggested.

"I'm afraid that wouldn't work," Jupiter

said. "His name might change, but his finger-prints would stay the same. Fingerprints have been used for over a hundred twenty-five years to identify people. So though it's a tempting theory, it simply can't be true."

"I cannot believe my husband knew this man," Dora Pelletier said, shaking her head.

"I wouldn't worry about it, Mrs. Pelletier," Jupiter said. "I expect your husband's only crime was going to high school with André Laurent. When the authorities almost caught him for counterfeiting in Massachusetts, he had to run. But before he left, he stabbed his partner in the heart and took his engraving plates.

"He had to find somewhere to go — and quickly — and he remembered his old friend from Montreal. He wrote down his name and address on an index card and made his way out west. I think he came to Jackson hoping to convince your husband to go into counterfeiting with him, and to find a place to set up shop. The newspaper article about the murder was a threat; the five hundred dollar bills were proof of his artistry; and the picture from St. John's Academy was to remind your husband of what good friends they'd been. And they were both French-Canadian."

"That is nothing to base a friendship or anything else on," Mrs. Pelletier said.

"I agree," Jupiter said. "Nevertheless, André Laurent seems drawn to old acquaintances. Since Spiridon Marcovic is dead, perhaps Laurent is now looking for his co-conspirator, the banker. It's too bad we have no idea where he is."

"But we do know where he is," Dora Pelletier said.

"What?" Pete said.

"Yes, indeed," John Pelletier said. "He's no longer a banker, of course, but he's still a prominent member of the community. After he was acquitted, he changed his name from Mihailo Ivanisevic and, five or six years later, he bought a number of vineyards that border each other. In fact, he's our next-door neighbor. His name is now Michael Ivan and he owns Dragutin Wines."

"What?" Pete exploded. "Then the man who laundered André Laurent's counterfeit cash has invited Branko's family to a Fourth of July celebration tonight! We're all going to be there!"

"We're going to be there, too," Dora said, smiling.

Just at that moment, Luke and Harper

came running inside, fast.

"I think we saw him!" cried Harper. "The man who dropped the bag with the paper in it!"

"He wasn't looking for water this time," Luke added. "He was in our field, not our neighbor's, and when we looked out to see where Penny and Zoey were, he was standing right next to them."

"We didn't know who he was right away, of course," clarified Harper. "But we went out to see what he wanted, and when we got closer, we saw that he was rubbing Penny's ear."

"When he saw us, he just asked if we'd found a bag with some paper in it," Luke added.

"We told him we hadn't seen it, and he walked away, waving," Harper said. "But he was wearing a *really* big hunting knife in a sheath on his right leg!"

10

No Fingerprints

The whole time Luke and Harper were talking, Bob and the others sat quietly, but as Harper got to the climax of the story, Pete and Branko both jumped to their feet.

"Where is he?" Pete yelled, and "Is he still here?" and "Let's go get him!"

Jupiter also rose, but only to lift the Boston *Globe* article off the desk and show it to the twins.

"Is this the man you saw?" he asked. Both Luke and Harper studied the photograph for quite a while before Luke said, somewhat doubtfully, "I'm not sure."

"It *could* have been. *Maybe,*" Harper added.

As for the man in the field, he was gone, and, soon afterwards, Bob and his friends were leaving, too. They had to get back to help with the cookout and to greet Worthington when he returned from Rocky Beach − though they were all having some trouble putting out of their minds the image of what Harper had described as a really big knife in a sheath.

In fact, when they got back to the bunkhouse, they found themselves discussing that knife, at some length. Jupiter pointed out that, if it *was* a hunting knife, as Harper had reported, it would be hard to stab anyone in the heart with it, and Pete said he'd recently learned that carrying daggers was illegal in California, so probably Laurent was stuck with a hunting knife for his killing nowadays.

"What makes a dagger different from a hunting knife?" Branko asked.

"A dagger has a really sharp point and two sharp edges," Jupiter explained.

Bob remained silent on the subject – though he thought about it nonetheless. He was glad when Worthington pulled into the Petrovic's driveway and unbundled himself from the Flex. He had obviously taken special care washing it, and the chimera decal was still intact. The dragon, lion, and ram looked brilliantly detailed and colorful, defiant and strong – ready to take on all comers, Bob thought.

A few hours later, Worthington and The Three Investigators joined the Petrovic family for the promised American-style cookout. The table was set with a red-white-and-blue tablecloth and there were blue and red streamers hung between the trees. Mrs. Petrovic had made potato salad, a Jell-O mold with crushed pineapple, cole slaw, and strawberry shortcake, and Mr. Petrovic grilled corn on the cob and hot dogs.

After the meal, Mrs. Petrovic finally agreed to the boys' repeated request that they be allowed to help, and she surrendered her kitchen to them, laughing.

"Such good boys," she said. "Your parents can be proud."

Now Bob and Jupiter were working together, while Branko and Pete formed a second team. Jupiter stood at the sink, looking out the kitchen window at a perfect picture of family contentment. Mrs. Petrovic sat under the trees with her husband, Milena beside her and Zivko cross-legged on the ground, playing with Zeus.

Jupiter's expression was indecipherable, and Bob wondered how he felt. Even Bob, who had perfectly good parents, envied the fact that Branko had a brother and a sister. But then, he reminded himself, he had Jupiter and Pete.

Pete and Branko had swept the kitchen floor, put away the leftovers, wiped down the counters, and proceeded to the yard, where Bob could see them chopping wood to replenish the supply that Mr. Petrovic had burned. Bob and Jupiter had loaded the Petrovics' dishwasher and now had turned to the cooking pots and the serving dishes.

"What do you plan to say to Michael Ivan tonight?" Bob said. "You asked John Pelletier to introduce us, didn't you?"

"I don't know precisely," Jupiter said. "But I'd like to offer him our help, if he wants it. After all, it surely crossed his mind that it might have been Laurent who broke into the wine cave, and if so, he must be feeling a bit uneasy; he may even know what Laurent was looking for. If we're to help, I need more information."

"But why do you want to help him?" Bob asked, truly curious. "This is the man who destroyed your family!"

By this time Jupiter had made it clear that he believed the family tree Bob had created was factual and not fictional. And Michael Ivan was the man who had blackmailed Jupiter's own grandfather Spiridon into helping a counterfeiter and who had probably also caused his early death.

"It's amazing to me that you don't seem angry or resentful," Bob added when Jupiter looked at him in surprise. "If it hadn't been for Michael Ivan, the women you think were your grandmother and mother wouldn't have had to

go into the witness protection program when
André Laurent jumped bail. Your mother
would never have changed her name. And
she'd probably own Dragutin Wines!"

Not only was Bob incensed on Jupiter's
behalf, but he found the entire story very upset-
ting. Spiridon Markovic had been born in a
displaced persons camp in Yugoslavia after
World War II, and his parents had brought
him to America in order to escape the kind of
arm-twisting and coercion they feared under a
Communist dictatorship. Bob's mother's parents had fled China for the very same reason,
but their story had had a happier ending. They
had never been blackmailed or coerced after
they came to America.

Spiridon, however, had been. He had
merely tried to realize his ambitions in a country that usually rewarded hard work and perse-
verance. He had saved his money; he had
bought a vineyard and made a success of it; he
had named his vineyard "precious." And then,
in a period of runaway inflation and soaring interest rates, he had made the mistake of trying
to expand. And everything had come crashing
down around him.

"What you say may indeed be true," Jupiter said, "and I am sure I will never be fond

of the man. But I bear him no ill will. After all, he, too, was a victim of André Laurent. I suppose he may have been guilty of a kind of predatory lending when he worked at the bank, but he did nothing that wasn't done all the time then. As for the money-laundering he engaged in, and the coercion of Spiridon Markovic – well, if Laurent hadn't threatened to burn down St. Sava's, Michael Ivan would never have done those things. He felt he had no choice."

"Why didn't he go to the police?" Bob asked.

"I can only imagine that the threat to burn down St. Sava's was one of many," Jupiter said. "No doubt he also threatened to kill Michael Ivan's loved ones. If André Laurent had stabbed his own partner to death back in Massachusetts, then no doubt Michael Ivan believed he would do exactly what he said he would."

That sounded all too plausible to Bob. Any man who could stab his own partner to the heart was a man it would be best to placate. He brought the last of the pots and cooking utensils to the sink.

"I'll take over," he said. "You've done enough washing."

Jupiter rinsed his hands and dried them

on a dishtowel. "It's also important to remember," he said, "that Mihailo Ivanisevic – or Michael Ivan – was tried by a jury of his peers and found innocent. They knew he was technically guilty of what the authorities had charged him with, but in a larger sense they clearly felt he wasn't guilty – that the degree of coercion he experienced had given him no choice.

"When it comes to the law, being able to make a choice matters greatly. The jury must have felt that the federal authorities had been trying to make Michael Ivan a scapegoat for the sins of someone else," he added.

"It's strange that you'd mention scapegoats," Bob said. "Mallory MacLeod just told me where the word comes from, and now that I've met Penny and Zoey, I think it's awful that Jewish priests cast innocent goats out into the wilderness for nothing they'd done themselves."

Bob could see that the mention of Mallory's name had momentarily distracted Jupiter.

"By the way," Bob said, "I think it was great that you invited Mallory to join us up here for the Fourth. Though I have to say I was surprised."

"I was surprised as well," Jupiter said.

He'd gotten some soapsuds on the bridge of his nose and he brushed them away with his forearm. "Mallory told me that Leif had informed her that the project – as she called it – was finished, and for a moment I had no idea what she was talking about. When I realized she was referring to her own thank-you present, I got so flustered I invited her."

"Whatever you may think," Bob said, "you'd never have done that if you weren't starting to like her."

"That," said Jupiter, "is a debatable deduction."

As Bob washed the last few pots and pans, Jupiter returned to the previous subject. "It's curious and complicated," he said. "If Michael Ivan hadn't done what he did, my mother might never have left Jackson. I don't know exactly where or when or how my parents met, but I do know that my father taught at the University of Toronto. And if my mother hadn't been forced to change her identity and go into hiding with her mother, what are the chances she'd have wound up anywhere near there? She'd never have met my father, and I would never have been born."

Just then Branko and Pete came back to the kitchen. "We are ready to go to Dragutin,"

Branko said. "Do you want to get anything from the bunkhouse?"

Bob had everything he needed and so did Jupiter, so they waited while the rest of the family and Worthington got ready. Zivko made sure that Zeus was safely in the house, with a full bowl of water, and they were off – the Petrovics in their van and the four boys in the Flex, with Worthington at the wheel.

Bob was looking forward to the evening. The photographs on the website had made Dragutin Wines look very beautiful. Besides, they would get to meet the Ivans and see where the break-in had occurred, and he had always loved Fourth of July fireworks.

But then Jupiter said, "We should do what we do best tonight. Keep our eyes open. Investigate everything! And don't forget that Laurent is on the loose. There's no better place to lose yourself than in a crowd, and I have a funny feeling that Laurent might show up to-night, hoping to check things out himself."

"But how will we know it is him?" Branko asked. "Luke and Harper didn't think that the man they met looked much like the photo in the newspaper."

"Remember the cowboy boots," Jupiter said. "He'll be in his sixties, I would think.

Look for anyone who seems out of place or suspicious."

The sun hadn't yet begun to set when they arrived at the vineyard, and though it would be more than an hour before it was dark enough for the fireworks to begin, the place was already very crowded.

Bob didn't know how many people had been invited, but Mr. Petrovic had said that Ivan had invited not only his neighbors but the entire congregation of St. Sava's as well as a lot of other people from the town.

Worthington followed the PARKING signs to a big field already holding a large number of cars, and after he'd parked, Bob and the others got out of the Flex. They soon were joined by the Petrovics, and all of them walked down the field to Dragutin Wines' main compound.

Bob was amazed at how far into the distance the rows of grapevines stretched on their trellises. In person, the place was both grander and more imposing than it had seemed in the online photos. The vineyard's central buildings — the tasting room, the gift shop, the sheds where the grapes were pressed, the house itself – were painted immaculately white.

Stone retaining walls backed extensive flower borders filled with pink and purple petunias, hosts of white lilies, and blooming roses that perfumed the air. Gravel walking paths, lined with twinkling lights, passed under pergolas twined with flowering vines, and, at the end of one, was a grand pavilion with a cedar shake roof where weddings and receptions could be catered. It was quite an operation, Bob thought.

"Wow!" Pete said.

"Yes," Mr. Petrovic said. "Michael Ivan is a very successful man."

Soon he and his wife were greeting friends and neighbors, and Bob and his friends thought it would be polite to leave them to it. After telling Worthington they'd look forward to seeing him later, they wandered around the central gravel courtyard. Long tables with white tablecloths had been set up, laden with cheeses and salted nuts and punchbowls full of lemonade and wine punch. Lanterns on thin wires glowed overhead. The yard was full of people talking and laughing.

As they neared the entrance to the gift shop, Jupiter suggested they go inside. The shop had double glass doors on which a large blue and white decal in the shape of a shield was prominently displayed. It boasted that the premises were surveilled twenty-four hours a day by a local Jackson security company. Bob imagined alarms and sirens and a rush of armed guards if the building was breached.

Jupiter noticed the sticker too, and when they were inside, he pointed out some of the system's details.

"The windows are separately wired," Jupiter said, "so if they're opened or broken after the system is armed, the sirens go off. It even looks as though there are pressure-sensitive pads on the floor. And look at all the security cameras!"

"Michael Ivan's taking no chances," Bob said.

"You can say that again," Pete said.

Bob wandered off to see what the gift shop was selling. He was surprised there was no wine, but Jupiter said that would be sold in the tasting room. Instead there were wine glasses and barware, books on viniculture and the history of Amador County, sweatshirts and t-shirts with "Dragutin Wines" printed on them – just about anything a tourist might buy on an impulse.

However, there was a section of the shop where things weren't for sale; in fact, it seemed to Bob more like a miniature museum. It reminded him a bit of the wall in Gordon Small's café on which he'd mounted the things he'd found in the attic, but here, everything had been carefully curated. On a piece of poster-board under thick plexiglass was the history of each piece – a small wooden handmade grape crusher, a collection of grape-harvesting bill-hook knives – which gave the display a continuity in both time and the wine-making process.

To Bob, the most interesting item was an old wine barrel, quite big, with a lot of bold black stenciling on the oak staves. It sat on its own pedestal, like a kind of altar, in the middle of the mini-museum. On both the front and back of the barrel, in prominent block lettering, the stenciling read DRAGUTIN WINES and SPIRIDON MARCOVIC and 1995. Red wax had been carefully applied all around the top edge of the barrel, an unbroken seal, and the wax was decorated with red ribbons and imprinted with what looked like a family crest. Whatever had been sealed in the barrel to begin with was clearly still in there.

"Come look at this!" Bob called to the rest of them, and soon the other three were reading the barrel's history with him. It was mounted on a stand-alone iron stand next to it.

According to the history, the barrel contained part of the trunk, roots, and many of the twining stems and leaves of a single grapevine – sealed in the barrel in 1995 to celebrate an extraordinary harvest. The article said this was an ancient Serbian custom to ensure record harvests in the future.

Bob found himself a bit skeptical. From what he'd seen of the grapevines at Cornucopia, not much of one would fit inside a barrel this size. But maybe that's what the custom intended — that the part stand for the whole. Still, it seemed like an odd thing to do — to rip a grapevine out of the earth and put it in a barrel.

"Have you ever heard of anything like this?" he asked Branko. "If it's a Serbian custom, you'd probably know."

"I have not heard of such a custom, no," Branko said, "but that does not mean there isn't one. Remember, it says an ancient Serbian custom, and I am not ancient."

Bob laughed. "But your father never did anything like this after a good harvest."

"No," Branko said. "I do not think he would destroy a producing vine."

"Maybe it's sort of like a scapegoat," Bob said. "Like a sacrifice to the god of wine."

"Such a sacrifice was not uncommon in ancient times," Jupiter agreed, "when the gods were deemed capricious and staying on their good side was very important. Nevertheless, I have to agree with Branko. It makes little sense that in modern times a vineyard owner would destroy a perfectly good vine out of a sort of superstition."

"I don't know," Pete said. "Superstitions can be pretty powerful."

Bob saw John Pelletier making his way toward them through the throngs in the gift shop. "Jupiter!" Mr. Pelletier called. "I've found Michael Ivan and I'm happy to introduce you. But he told me he's so busy tonight that all he'll have time for is a quick hello."

Jupiter turned to Pete and Branko. "Now remember what I said before: keep your eyes wide open. Bob and I will meet Mr. Ivan and see what we can discover."

Bob and Jupiter followed Mr. Pelletier out of the gift shop and across the courtyard to where Mr. Ivan was discussing the procedures for the fireworks with a man who turned out to be the foreman at Dragutin. As he and Jupiter waited for him to be done, Bob tried to get a sense of him.

Michael Ivan seemed a shy man – looking older than he should have, perhaps bowed down by troubles. His hair was graying and his face was worn, but he seemed kind, and as he glanced around at his neighbors, Bob could feel his desire that everyone have a good time.

The fact that he'd invited so many people to the event suggested his community spirit, and Bob already knew of his devotion to St. Sava's. It was what had made him vulnerable to the depredations of André Laurent in the first place, and it seemed ironic that his love for his church had driven him into crime.

Mr. Pelletier brought the boys over. "Michael," he said to Mr. Ivan, "I'd like you to meet some young friends of mine. This is Jupiter Jones and Bob Andrews, two of The Three Investigators. I'll leave you alone with them."

Mr. Ivan smiled a bit halfheartedly and had some trouble meeting Bob's gaze. His handshake was less than firm. "I'm pleased to meet you," he said, "but as I said to John, I'm afraid I have no time right now to speak with you at any length."

"I understand," Jupiter said. "I just had a quick question, if you'd be so kind. We heard about the break-in here the other night. Do you have any idea who it might have been?"

"No," Michael Ivan said. He looked away, and Bob couldn't tell if he was being truthful. "The whole thing seems so senseless.

There's nothing in the wine cave but barrels of wine. I called the police, but they couldn't find anything. But I have an excellent security system on the house, office, and gift shop, so I'm not worried about future trouble. If anyone triggered an alarm, armed guards would be here in five minutes."

"Yes, we saw the stickers and the wires," Jupiter said. "Nevertheless, if we can be of any assistance to you – " He reached in his pocket and presented Mr. Ivan with one of their business cards.

"Thank you," Ivan said. "I'm truly sorry I have to go. Tomorrow my wife Sarah and I will have a lot of digging out to do from this affair. But perhaps you could come back on Tuesday for a proper visit? I'd welcome it. And please bring young Branko Petrovic. I haven't met him yet, though I know his parents and brother and sister from St. Sava's."

He and his foreman went off, presumably to check on the fireworks, and Jupiter and Bob headed back toward the gift shop. They hadn't gotten far across the gravel yard before Pete and Branko rushed up. Pete was red-faced and so excited he could hardly speak; his mouth opened and closed and he hopped from foot to foot. Branko looked like he'd seen a ghost.

"Calm down!" Jupiter said. "What happened?"

"It was him!" Pete said. Branko nodded fiercely. "We were near the counter where the lights are so bright – "

"There are spotlights right above the cash register," Branko explained.

" — and it was so crowded," Pete went on. "We couldn't even hear each other. We almost had to yell. Then someone bumped into us from behind, and when we turned to see who it was – "

"It was a man," Branko said. "He threw his hands up in the air like this." Branko demonstrated, palms up and out and at shoulder level, as if he were surrendering. "Like he was saying sorry. But he had a weird smile on his face."

"And he had no fingerprints!" Pete said. "The pads of his fingers were all scarred and gnarly, like he had burned them in a fire or with acid."

"Very ugly," Branko said. "We both saw it."

"And then he turned and walked away and we looked down and – "

"Let me guess," Jupiter said. "He was

wearing cowboy boots!"

"Yes!" Pete said. "With pointed toes! He's off somewhere in the crowd right now. He didn't look like his school picture, but he looked a little like the photograph in the Boston *Globe*. And he looked like a murderer, that's for sure."

"Sinister," Branko agreed.

"Dangerous," Pete said. "Although at least he didn't have a knife!"

"Do you remember what you were saying just before he bumped into you?" Jupiter asked.

"Yes," Branko said. "I was telling Pete how much I liked working on a case with The Three Investigators, and how great it was to have you visit Cornucopia Wines and stay with me in the bunkhouse."

"And you were yelling this, in order to be heard above the noise?" Jupiter asked

"It was so loud in there, we had to," said Pete.

"So it's logical to assume that André Laurent heard you − that he now knows who we are, and where we're staying?"

"Oh no!" Branko said. "That might be true!"

"It really might!" Pete said.

"Still, what you saw explains our earlier

puzzlement," Jupiter said thoughtfully. "At the time Laurent was arrested in Jackson, there was no facial recognition software, and when he jumped bail, he must have decided that the safest way to protect himself from being re-arrested was to burn his fingerprints off.

"At some point after he did that, it seems likely he was arrested for a different crime. To coin a phrase, Pete was right on the money when he said that if Laurent was in prison, he must be there under a different name," Jupiter concluded.

"So he *has* been locked up all these years for another crime, and has just been released!" said Pete.

"That would seem the most likely explanation for the facts as we know them so far," Jupiter said.

"Maybe we can find him in the crowd, and point him out to you," Branko said. "But from a really safe distance."

"Come on. Let's get looking," Pete agreed.

Branko grabbed Pete's arm and led the way, while Bob and Jupiter followed. By now, the sun had set and it was getting darker. It wouldn't be long before the fireworks started, Bob thought.

Slowly the crowd was moving toward the field where they would be held, and as the boys got away from the strings of mini-lights, it became harder and harder to see peoples' faces. Bob saw Pete start, once or twice — thinking he'd seen Laurent — but it was a false alarm, and in the end, they all concluded that André Laurent was nowhere to be found.

"He'll turn up," Jupiter said. "Like a bad penny."

"Or a bad one hundred dollar bill," Bob said.

"Though I bet he's feeling pretty good right around now," Pete said.

"What do you mean?" Bob asked.

"I mean, he's fresh out of prison," Pete said, "and it's the Fourth of July!"

"I get it!" Branko said. "Independence Day!"

"Ha ha!" Pete crowed, clapping his hands.

"I hope he celebrates while he can, because whatever he may be planning, we're going to stop him, and get him," Jupiter said.

11

A Red Letter Fourth of July

The minute these words were out of Jupiter's mouth, he half regretted having said them. It was one thing to make a resolution to accomplish a certain end, and something else entirely to sound more certain about your chance of doing so than you really were.

Still, when he had opened his mouth to say what he had said, he had merely been trying to rally the troops – and in that, at least, it appeared he had succeeded, because as he and the others walked back toward the gravel courtyard, Branko, Pete, and Bob were talking about André Laurent, and in the flush of his previously successful impersonation, Branko threw his hands up again in mock surprise, egged on by Pete's and Bob's nervous laughter.

Jupiter, while faintly amused, knew his friends were only horsing around in order to mask their feelings of apprehension. André Laurent had now taken physical form and he was, as Pete might have put it, a scary dude. Jupiter himself stood off to the side, thinking hard about the case. At the horizon, the western sky was streaked with bands of rose and tangerine, shading to royal blue higher up. Jupiter estimated that it would still take a while before it would be dark enough for the fireworks to begin.

He'd had a hunch that Laurent would show up at Dragutin that evening, and now he was trying to figure out exactly why. Obviously Laurent was neither a patriot nor a fan of fireworks, and his appearance in public was both brazen and risky. There was always the chance that someone would recognize him, even after twenty-five years.

The wine cave, of course, was not connected to Michael Ivan's extensive and expensive security system, and whoever had broken in had had all the time he'd needed to look for what he was after. If it had been André Laurent — and who else could it logically have been? — then he hadn't found what he'd been looking for, or else he'd be long gone by now, far away from Jackson.

Instead, he was still on the prowl, and tonight he'd have a far better chance of finding what he was looking for while hiding in plain sight in the crowds. From what Pete and Branko had told him, the man radiated menace and would immediately have stood out on a regular business day. Jupiter paused and stared at the gift shop, where Laurent had last been seen. It was closed now, in preparation for the fireworks; its interior lights were dimmed. But a bank of spotlights flooded the front double-glass doors, and Jupiter again saw the blue security shield.

If what Laurent was looking for was in the gift shop, he clearly understood the danger. Breaking in would immediately trigger sirens, police, and security guards. Obviously he'd have wanted to case the joint in order to see if a break-in was feasible. Jupiter had to admit he'd have done the same thing: these crowds were a perfect cover for Laurent's reconnaissance.

Jupiter had been pinching his lip, and now he pinched it harder. In the minutes after the first sighting, he and his friends had looked everywhere for Laurent, but he was nowhere to be found. It seemed somewhere between possible and likely that Laurent had discovered what he was looking for in the gift shop and now had left the property to figure out his next move. So what could he be after? It would have to be something he'd known about when he first fled Jackson, something that went back to 1995 —

something he might first have broken into a wine cave to look for. Something, Jupiter thought suddenly, like the barrel marked with Spiridon Markovic's name, and the date 1995.

But that held only a solitary sacrificial grapevine. Or did it? Was it possible that it held something else? Like – for example — money printed in the Dragutin cave? The red wax seals on the barrel had never been broken, and if Jupiter's probable grandfather was the only person (other than Laurent) who knew it contained counterfeit money, then that money might still be there – and Laurent might be after it.

How much would it weigh? Let's say there were two million dollars in $100 bills, Jupiter thought. He remembered from his reading that the U.S Treasury claimed that every bill, no matter its denomination, weighed a single gram, and there were about 450 grams in a pound. He thought, with a faint smile, that he ought to remember this puzzle and give it to Uncle Titus the next time they met.

Assuming the bills were uniformly one hundred dollars each, there would be twenty thousand of them in two million dollars. Twenty thousand grams would equal about forty-four pounds. If Laurent were lucky and fast, he could simply break open the barrel, thrust the money in a backpack, and take off with it before the security guards arrived. In one way, Jupiter hoped Laurent would do just that. He was indeed a dangerous and probably desperate man, and the sooner he was gone from the scene, the sooner everyone would be safe.

But Jupiter doubted he would take the chance. The security system was too good, the guards too close — and armed, to boot. Michael Ivan had said they'd be on the scene in five minutes. No, André Laurent might be desperate, but he was smarter than that — and if he *had* located an old stash of counterfeit money but decided he couldn't safely steal it, then by now he had moved on to another plan.

Jupiter had always been more than a little surprised at how easily his own logic and intelligence could be applied to criminal endeavors, but, after all, he always reassured himself, criminals were human beings too — and deduction went hand in hand with an understanding of human nature. So, Jupiter thought, I can't get at the barrel of easy money, and my generator isn't working so I can't start up my printing press. Logically, I'd want to retrieve my engraved plates so I could start up again somewhere new. With that realization, Jupiter was flooded with an acute sense of unease. The engraved plates were hidden in the bunkhouse at Cornucopia Wines.

Well, at least there was no way Laurent could know for sure who had taken the plates or where they were – if indeed he decided to go back to the cave, and, there, discovered that the plates were missing. He might now know that some boys who called themselves The Three Investigators were staying in the bunkhouse at Cornucopia Wines, but he would have no reason to suspect that they had taken his plates. Or would he? Jupiter remembered emerging into the cavern and Pete and Branko saying something —

Jupiter was startled to hear Worthington's voice.

"There you are," he called as he materialized out of the gathering darkness and strode across the gravel toward the four boys.

"Worthington!" Pete said. "Where have you been?"

"Preparing for the evening's festivities," Worthington said. "The Pelletiers and Petrovics have laid out blankets on a premier spot of grassy field facing the spot from which the rockets will be launched, and I've been dispatched to round the four of you up to get you to join us."

"Lead on!" Branko said. "We will follow."

Pete walked next to Worthington, talking to him, Branko and Bob close behind. Jupiter hung back a little. He was still thinking. The crowd was dense when they got to the field, and Jupiter was glad there was still some daylight left, or else threading their way among and between the various encampments of friends and families would have been a tricky business.

There must have been over two hundred people there, in low camp chairs and sitting on blankets, with coolers and baskets of food. The mood was festive. Everywhere he looked, Jupiter saw smiling faces, and laughter floated in the evening air. It was good to be among so many friendly people on the Fourth of July.

The Pelletiers and Petrovics had found a fine spot near the back of the field, and the two families mingled together on three large blankets. Zivko and Luke seemed to be inseparable. Mr. and Mrs. Petrovic were talking with Mrs. Pelletier, and as Worthington and the boys chose spots to sit, Jupiter found himself sitting near John Pelletier, his mother Dora, and Harper.

"Hello, Harper," Jupiter said. "I hope your goats have recovered from their encounter with their unexpected visitor. Do Zoey and Penny like fireworks?"

Harper looked up at him with interest. "I don't really know," she said. "But it's past their bedtime, anyway."

Jupiter relaxed and lay back with his eyes closed, but when he heard someone say the name "Spiridon," he sat up and paid better attention. It turned out that John and Dora Pelletier were talking about Dragutin Wines.

"It has changed so much," Dora said, "since the old days. Back when Spiridon and Nadja owned it, it was just a small family vineyard."

"But successful," John said. "They did very well before the bad things happened."

"Now it is too big, I think," Dora said, "with so much emphasis on things other than wine-making – the weddings, the group tours. I heard Ivan is thinking of a small hotel."

"Yes," John Pelletier said. "A bed and breakfast, if the planning commission agrees."

"I do not begrudge him his success,"

Dora said. "Well, maybe a little. After all, his fortune is partly based on the misfortune of others. Back when the Markovics owned Dragutin, too many vineyards overextended themselves at a time when inflation was very high, and Michael Ivan signed off on some of the loans – and when it came to Dragutin, asked a high price for restructuring theirs. Even though he lost his job at the bank after the trial, he still made a lot of money in the stock market and managed to get out before the big crash."

As Jupiter listened to this recapitulation of information he already knew, he was also looking at Harper – who didn't seem to be listening at all. In fact, she was earnestly writing in her notebook, intent on getting whatever it was as close to perfect as possible.

"What are you working on?" Jupiter asked her.

"Oh," she said, looking up at him, surprised. "I'm just rewriting some notes I made about sterilization and milk production earlier this afternoon."

Meanwhile, Mr. Petrovic got up from where he'd been sitting and joined them.

"I heard you talking about Michael Ivan," he said to the Pelletiers. "I agree with you that he took advantage of what he himself had helped to cause, but after he bought Dragutin Wines, he must still have been feeling guilty about everything that had happened, because he has had this Fourth of July celebration every year since then."

Jupiter found listening to adults converse about ideas restful – even ideas about monetary policy. As much as he loved Aunt Mathilda and Uncle Titus, they rarely sat around discussing ideas. His uncle was always rushing off to investigate a new auction, and his aunt was busy with the ins and outs of a daily business.

The conversation had now broadened to the American Revolution – which made sense, after all. As Dora Pelletier pointed out, today was the celebration of the signing of the Declaration of Independence. Both Mr. Pelletier and his mother seemed well versed in American history, though Mr. Petrovic had some catching up to do.

"I understand, of course," he said, "the desire to govern yourself and not be forced to do things by someone else. But why did those people throw tea into the ocean?"

Soon everyone in both families was talking about the causes of the revolution, correcting misimpressions and misinformation. It was all about taxes, wasn't it? Pete said. No taxation without representation? Well, yes, Bob said. But before that, it was about war. The British thought the people living in their American colonies ought to help pay for the French and Indian War – which it asserted had been waged to protect the colonists from the French-Canadians.

"Whoa! French Canadians!" Pete said.

"Yes," said Bob, "but the colonists believed that the British had fought the French and Indian War to protect their empire, not to help the colonists, and they thought it was unfair to make them pay when the people who taxed them were British and had no understanding of what it was like to live across the ocean!"

There was a tax on tea, Dora Pelletier told Mr. Petrovic, and when a bunch of tea was sent from England to America, the colonists refused to let it be unloaded and instead ruined it by throwing it in Boston Harbor.

"Well, to be fair," Mr. Pelletier said, "there was a long list of grievances, all of them listed in the Declaration of Independence. But the Founding Fathers were also forward-thinking men who believed in life, liberty, and the pursuit of happiness. That's why America be-

223

came the place it did — a place people all over the world came to when they wanted either freedom from oppression, or just the freedom to work, raise a family, and be happy."

He seemed about to say something more when suddenly, out of the gathering darkness, Jupiter heard a whoosh, and he turned to see that the first aerial rocket was streaking upward into the blue-black sky, trailed by a thin tail of smoke.

Up, up it went, until it was directly overhead, and then it exploded, sending out from its center what seemed to Jupiter like hundreds of white stars before they faded and the sky was black again.

Along with all the others, Jupiter couldn't help himself. "Ooohh," he said, in awe.

"Here we go!" Pete said.

There was a pause and Jupiter could tell that the crowd's excitement had ratcheted up a notch. And they weren't disappointed.

The next rocket was a brilliant gold chrysanthemum, its hundreds of stars leaving trails of sparks behind as they exploded from the center. He looked to his right and in the burst of light saw the happiness on Dora Pelletier's face. She sat between Jupiter and Harper, and she reached out and impulsively took Harper's hand. Between the booms, twirling sparkles, and swirls of color, she began talking about her childhood.

"Oh," she said, "we loved fireworks so much when I was a girl, when the whole family was still together. My older sister and I were so close. She was very smart − a young scientist − and she couldn't resist explaining everything to me − about gunpowder and the metal salts and iron filings that make the colors and the sparkles. She was so serious. Like you, Harper."

Harper smiled at her. Another rocket shot up, and to Jupiter it seemed to keep exploding and exploding, sending showers of sparks and trailing smoke until it covered the entire sky.

"She loved the sky," Dora Pelletier said. "Not only these — " she gestured upwards — "but the fireworks of the heavens themselves. She got a telescope one Christmas and we often looked at the stars at night. If we stayed out too long and didn't go to bed, my father would joke that the Black Hand would get us."

Jupiter was wrenched out of his fireworks trance as he turned to look at her in mild surprise.

"The Black Hand?" he said.

"Yes," Dora Pelletier said, "a secret Serbian society, now long gone. It is a scary name, no? Enough to frighten a child. But it was a joke, and we knew it. My grandfather had been the nephew of a man who was in the Black Hand back in the old country, before he came to America."

Another rocket went off, painting the sky in brilliant colors, and then another – a chrysanthemum so gigantic its outward stars seemed so close Jupiter thought he could have reached up and grabbed one.

The fireworks display was heating up. The rockets were being set off more quickly now. Barely had the light and noise of one faded before another took its place. There were more peonies and chrysanthemums and willows with their trailing streaks of fire, as well as fireworks within fireworks, cascading stars of pink and blue, each setting off another small explosion. Jupiter's pulse was racing.

"And then, of course, my sister got married to the man who owned the vineyard across the street, and had her lovely daughter, who resembled her so much. Robert and I used to visit them just by taking a walk across the road."

Once again, Jupiter's focus on the fireworks was interrupted. What could Mrs. Pelletier mean about visiting her sister just by taking a walk across the road? He was about to ask her, when she added, "And then came the tragedy."

Dora Pelletier was lost in reminiscence – carried away into the past – but Jupiter was getting more and more tense.

"What tragedy?" he asked.

Dora Pelletier looked at him, surprised. "Well, maybe it wasn't a tragedy," she said. "Maybe it all turned out fine in the end. Well, not fine. My sister died. But although I never heard from my niece again after she and her mother had to leave California, the last I heard, she was attending Cornell and studying astronomy."

"Astronomy?" Jupiter asked. "At Cornell?" Now his pulse was really racing, but it had little to do with the fireworks. Along with his pulse, his mind was racing, too, putting together the pieces of another puzzle – one that had stumped him for years. The sky was dark again for a few seconds, and Jupiter understood this was the lull before the storm, the gathering expectation before the grand finale.

"If I may ask you, Mrs. Pelletier," he said. "What was your sister's name – and what was *your* last name before you married your husband?"

In the hush, her voice was clear and strong. "My sister was Nadja and our last name was Dimitrijevic. We were Nadja and Dorajeta Dimitrijevic. When she married, my sister's name was Markovic. Her daughter's name was Aleksandrina. We called her Xandra."

The finale began, one rocket following another in quick succession, the sky filling with color, explosions of blue and green, red and white, trailing sparks of gold and silver, brilliant coruscations coming so fast together they took Jupiter's breath away. The crowd was oohing and ahhing in rapture, and the resulting booms were a deafening battery of noise in which Jupiter could hardly think.

Still, think he did. The pieces had finally locked in place. He was watching the conclusion of the Fourth of July fireworks in Jackson, California with his grandmother's sister. Dora Pelletier – née Dimitrijevic – was his mother's aunt, and his own great-aunt; her son John was Jupiter's first cousin once removed, and his children Luke and Harper were Jupiter's second cousins. Where he had least expected them, he had found the missing half of his family.

His breath caught in his throat. He wasn't used to emotion this strong, and he wasn't sure what to do with it. The smell of gunpowder was heavy in the air. The reverberations were dying away, and as the smoke began to clear, the night sky was becoming visible again. Somewhere out there was a planet named Jupiter and a galaxy his father had named after his mother.

Even though he was sitting down, Jupiter felt shaky as well as thrilled and overwhelmed. Forget his red chalk – this had become a red letter Fourth of July. He turned to Dora Pelletier.

"I really don't know how to say this," he said, "but your niece Aleksandrina Markovic was almost certainly my mother."

12

A Knife in the Dark

Pete had been so excited and amazed at what had happened the night before that he'd hardly slept at all. After he and the others had gotten back to the bunkhouse, he'd lain in the dark as images flashed in his mind. André Laurent with no fingerprints! Jupiter hugging his great-aunt! Pete had never seen a man with no fingerprints before, but then again he had also never seen Jupiter hug anyone like that – not once in the nine years he'd known him.

Now it was morning and Pete sat groggily at the table in the bunkhouse, slowly waking up. Worthington had asked the boys the night before if they'd need the Flex in the morning, and when they'd said they wouldn't, he'd said he'd like to visit the man he used to drive for in Jackson. He was probably on his way there now, Pete thought. The Petrovics, along with Zivko and Milena, had left for the day, having to drive back to Sonoma to deal with details about the sale of the house there.

The boys had Cornucopia Wines to themselves. Branko had brought cereal and

230

fruit back from the main house and the four of them now sat together eating breakfast.

"I still cannot believe this," Branko said to Jupiter. "Not only are you Serbian, but you are related to our good friends!"

"Only half Serbian," Jupiter reminded him. "Welsh on my father's side."

"Nevertheless," said Branko. "A whole new family."

Jupiter smiled and then resumed eating. Pete looked at him closely, trying to figure out how he felt this morning. The evening before had certainly been one to remember. After Jupiter had made his announcement to Dora Pelletier, it seemed everyone had held their breath for a moment, and then, as the crowd got to its feet after the fireworks, questions and explanations had come tumbling out.

Jupiter had explained about his birth certificate and the research that Bob had done — about discovering that his father had named a galaxy Xandra, about his prior deductions about the name change, and so on — and soon Dora Pelletier, her face aglow, was hugging Jupiter and he was hugging her back. And not only her. Jupiter had also hugged John and Harper and Luke!

The feeling of enthusiasm had been so

infectious that soon everybody was hugging everybody.

"It is good to have the whole story," Branko now said to Jupiter. "Yes?"

"Yes, indeed," Jupiter said. "I had figured out most of the larger pieces, but there were lots of details to fill in. Bob, maybe it's time to complete the Jones Family Tree."

Bob opened the genealogy website he'd used and went to the page Pete had seen before.

"Here I am at the bottom," Jupiter said, "and above me are my parents, Claudius Jones and Alexandrina Marcovic. Above my mother are *her* parents, Spiridon Marcovic and Nadja Dimitrijevic Marcovic. Now add Nadja's sister."

Bob drew a line to the left of Nadja and entered Dora Dimitrijevic Pelletier, and then connected the two of them to Dranko Dimitrijevic. He also put in Dora's French-Canadian husband and their son John, and his children Luke and Harper.

Pete could see it better now. Jupiter's father's family history was one thing, and his mother's was entirely different. On his father's side he was Welsh; on his mother's side he was Serbian.

"So clear!" Branko said. "My Serbian brother!"

Jupiter smiled.

The night before, Dora Pelletier had said that her sister Nadja – Jupiter's grandmother – hadn't told her much about the troubles at Dragutin as they were occurring, except that Ivanisevic was doing something at the bank to make things easier for her husband. None of the Pelletiers had known about the blackmail or the counterfeiting scheme and now Pete asked Jupiter to go over the whole thing again, so that he could remember it and tell his parents when they all got home.

"Well," said Jupiter. "For close to three years, Laurent was using the Dragutin side of the cave for his counterfeiting operation, and no one knew."

"It's even more amazing than that!" Bob said. "Until two days ago, no one other than Spiridon Markovic, André Laurent, and Michael Ivan even knew where Laurent had set up shop."

"Laurent had the perfect situation," Jupiter said. "He made fantastic counterfeit money and Ivanisevic exchanged it for real money at the bank. Of course, when my grandfather died so suddenly and unexpectedly, everything

233

changed. My grandmother went to her sister and told her what had happened, and together they decided that my grandmother should go to the authorities and expose the operation, hoping that helping them would keep her from getting punished herself."

"But she hadn't done anything!" Pete said, "Except be married to her husband – who was only trying to save the vineyard!"

"Yes," Jupiter said. "That's true."

"And she was ready to testify against the bad guys!" Pete added.

"Indeed, things might have worked out," Jupiter said, "if Laurent hadn't jumped bail. But he was such a dangerous and unpredictable character with such a violent past that, with him on the loose, my grandmother was terrified. The authorities were so concerned that Laurent might get to her before she testified that they put her in the witness protection program. So that's how her name and my mother's name got changed."

"And that's why they left Jackson," Bob said.

"This André Laurent has scared a lot of people," Branko said. "Dora Pelletier said that when her sister called her that one time to tell her your mother was in college at Cornell, she was still so worried about Laurent that she refused to tell her own sister what her new name was. And when Jupiter's mother called Dora to tell her that Nadja had died, that was the last time she heard anything about either of them."

"And all this time," Bob added, "Dora Pelletier was assuming that her niece was still alive and well."

"Yes," Jupiter said. "I must admit it was hard to see how sad they were when I told them my mother had died so many years ago. I'm sad as well, of course, but in a theoretical way, if that makes sense. I never even met her, but they knew her very well. She and John played together as children."

"It was good of your new family," Branko said, "to invite the four of us to dinner tonight."

"I'm sure there'll be much more talk about all of this," Jupiter said. "But I hope not *too* much more. I have to say I find it a little exhausting."

Pete smiled. Thinking too much or too hard was what got Pete exhausted, but it was different for Jupiter.

As for Pete, although he was looking forward to seeing Jupiter's family again, he was also looking forward to seeing Connor O'Malley – the artist The Three Investigators had met the last time they were in the Gold Country, who, as it turned out, was also a mentor for the local 4-H Club. For one thing, Pete genuinely liked him, and for another he'd had an idea he wanted to run by him – an idea inspired by the decal on the back of the Ford Flex.

Jupiter interrupted Pete's thoughts. "And that concludes, quite happily, the first of the cases we were following. But I'm afraid we haven't yet brought to an end the second – and dangerous – one," he said.

They'd finished their breakfast long before, and they all got up from the table together. Pete was now fully awake and ready for anything.

"I know you're thinking all the time, Jupe," he said. "So I bet you've come to some conclusions. But before you tell us, here's one I came to on my own." He paused and looked at his friends. "Yesterday this André Laurent character showed up twice – at the Pelletiers when we were visiting, and again at Dragutin last night, when Branko and I saw him. He's getting more and more reckless, and reckless people do unpredictable things. What's he going to do next, I wonder?"

"You're right, Pete," Jupiter said. "I do think he's gotten more desperate, and I think I know what he plans to do. Last night I concluded that when he discovered the generator was broken, he decided to try to locate a large stash of counterfeit money which I think is almost certainly in the barrel in the display section of the gift shop."

"I thought that only held an old grapevine!" Pete said.

"I believe that story about the grapevine was just a ruse," Jupiter said. "But I also think that Laurent has decided it would be too dangerous to try to break into the gift shop and grab the contents of the barrel. Tomorrow, when we go to Dragutin to talk to Mr. Ivan, I'll try to get him to break the red wax seal and see if my hypothesis is correct. I assume our criminal friend – "

"He's not our friend!" Pete said.

" – doesn't have a car, or anywhere to sleep other than in the cave. And he obviously has no money or he wouldn't be here in Jackson in the first place. So I've concluded he'll go to his lair and retrieve his counterfeiting plates so he can set up shop somewhere else."

"But the plates aren't in his shop any more," Pete said.

"I know," Jupiter said.

"Because we took them," Branko said.

"I know," Jupiter said. Pete watched him as he went to the room where the boys slept and, from underneath his own bunk, retrieved the suitcase with the engraved metal plates. He brought it back, sprung the latches, and opened the top.

Pete stared at the plates, which seemed to glimmer with malevolence.

"The last time you mentioned this I said there was no problem because Laurent didn't know who we are or where we are staying," Jupiter said. "Now, I'm not so sure."

"If I'm following Jupe," Bob said, "we have to assume that when the two of you – " He gestured to Pete and Branko " – were talking in the gift shop, Laurent heard you. He knows who we are and where we're staying. But why would he connect us to the plates? There'd be no reason to do that unless he saw us, or heard us, in the cave."

Uh oh, Pete thought. He remembered the uneasy feeling he'd had when they'd gotten to the Dragutin end of the cave – the sneeze he told himself couldn't have been a sneeze, the prickly sense that someone was watching or had been there recently.

In fact, when he and Branko had been coming out into the cavern, hadn't Branko said something about The Three Investigators? He told the others what he was afraid of.

Branko looked stricken, but Jupiter rushed to reassure him.

"It could have been any of us," he said. "Besides, how could you know? Still, if Laurent actually heard a mention of The Three Investigators, then went into the cavern and discovered that the plates were missing, he almost certainly knows who took them."

"Let's get them – and us – out of here right now!" Pete yelled. He slammed the suitcase closed and pushed in the latches.

"I think we should call the police," suggested Branko.

Pete thought so, too, but Bob, of all people, said, "I don't know. There are four of us – five with Worthington – and only one of him. Wouldn't it be better to catch him in the act, if he comes here?"

"But maybe he has a gun!" Pete said. "After all, we know he has a knife."

"Given the stringent California gun laws, it's highly unlikely that he has a gun already," Jupiter said. "Nevertheless – and whether or not we try to catch him in the act – I agree we should get the counterfeiting plates out of here."

"I know a great spot!" Pete said. "If Laurent thinks we took the plates from the cave, he sure wouldn't think we'd put them back there. Remember when I found that nook I said reminded me of the secret drawer at John Chang's? That's a perfect hiding place. What do you think?"

For once in his life, Jupiter looked uncertain. "I don't know," he said. "Though I agree with you that that would make an excellent hiding place, I feel as if there's something I should be considering that I'm not. Something about last night." He looked off into space. "Oh, well, let's do it. We'll have to be quick and very careful, though."

They packed their backpacks with their gear; Pete got the honor of carrying the plates, and Bob packed his cellphone and the GPS, as he always did, even when they weren't likely to be needed. But when they got back to the cave and started down the tunnel, following the red question marks that Jupiter had scrawled on the walls, Pete suddenly wondered if he'd had such a good idea after all. The fact was – as he'd already pointed out a day or so ago – he and caves had a pretty up-and-down relationship.

"Geez," he said. "I'm sure glad you decided to use your chalk, Jupe. I forgot how many side tunnels there are."

"Yes," Jupiter said, over his shoulder. "A tricky cave, indeed."

Tricky, Pete thought. And dark. Their headlamps and flashlights danced on the floor and wall in crazy patterns. Still, all in all, Pete felt pretty relaxed. At least this time they weren't going very far in, and soon they'd be back in the daylight.

They followed Jupe's question marks for about fifteen minutes, right to the little cavern he remembered, and, sure enough, the nook was perfect. It was a relief to get the plates out of his backpack. Jupiter was pleased with how well hidden they were.

"Done and dusted, as Worthington might say," said Bob. "Now let's get out of here."

"Let's leg it!" Pete said.

Jupiter led the way back, following his own careful markings. He was walking quickly, with Branko following. Bob was third, and Pete last, doing his best to keep up. He was surprised at how inky and tactile the darkness seemed; somehow the headlamps and flashlights stabbed through the blackness but didn't illuminate it.

The air was filled with the echoes of their footsteps and the raspy sound of their breathing – but as he walked at the end of the line of boys, Pete had the strangest impression that there were the sounds of footsteps coming up *behind* him. Of course, the sound must be merely an echo. Even so, it had an oddly irregular pattern – it seemed to stop, then go, then stop, then go again. Almost as if someone was following him, stopping, then following him again.

As Pete started to turn to reassure himself that he must be imagining all this, he heard a strange quick rushing noise, and then, without warning, out of the blackness, a strong arm whipped around his chest and pulled him backwards off his feet. Something cold pressed against his throat. The vinegary smell of sweat. A man's harsh whisper.

"Not a move," he said, "or I'll slit you from ear to ear." His breath was sour.

Pete went slack. It was a knife he felt, its chilly blade pressing against his jugular. He gulped. Ahead of him the other three boys heard the commotion and turned – almost blinding Pete with their flashlights.

"Get those lights out of my face," André Laurent said, his voice nasty and rough.

Instantly Jupiter, Bob, and Branko directed their lights down, toward the rock floor. In the glare of his own light Pete could see their faces – shocked, scared, and in the case of Jupiter, also strangely remorseful.

"The Three Investigators," Laurent said. "Where are my plates? I want them now. I know you were in my workshop. Don't fool around if you value your friend's life."

"His name is Pete," Jupiter said. "And since I'm the one who stupidly exposed him to your knife, why don't you let him go, and hold me instead?"

"Fat chance," Laurent said. "The really stupid thing was being in the cave this morning. I'm not going to say it again – give me the plates!" His voice had gotten louder and more threatening.

"They're in a side cavern about ten minutes back," said Jupiter. "We'll get them for you right away. Just don't hurt Pete."

"That will depend on you," Laurent said, pulling Pete roughly against the wall. He could feel the blade's sharp edge as his friends scrambled back up the passage toward where they'd hidden the plates. "Put your hands behind your back," Laurent ordered. "No funny business."

Pete did as he was told. Laurent grabbed Pete's hands and lifted, torquing Pete's shoulders. "Ow!" he yelled, dropping his flashlight. The man quickly sheathed his knife and forcefully tied Pete's wrists with a rope he took from his pocket. The flashlight rolled across the floor casting weird shadows everywhere. In no time Laurent was holding the knife again, its blade glinting in the light. He picked up the flashlight as Pete staggered backwards.

For the first time, Pete got a close look at him. The night before he'd been so shocked by the man's hands that he hadn't really looked at his face. Now he did. Laurent's hair was dirty blond and disheveled. His eyes were the light blue of ice, and he gave off a palpable sense of feral menace. He was shorter than Pete but he looked strong, and his fingerprintless fingers were stubby.

"You kids think you're smart," Laurent said. "You have no idea how easy it was for me to figure out who'd taken my plates."

"What do you mean?" Pete said.

"You gave yourselves away twice – in the cave and in the gift shop. And that black-haired kid even let me know where you're staying. I hope you like my company, because once I've got what I came for – and get a car – you'll be coming with me until I'm safe."

Why were people always grabbing him in caves? Pete wondered. He tried hard to keep calm – after all, getting all riled up would solve nothing – and found it oddly easy. He took deep breaths. Though he was easily spooked, he always felt calmer when there was real danger.

"I bet you're not such a bad guy, really," Pete said.

Laurent laughed harshly. "That's a bet you'd lose, kid," he said.

Pete took another tack. "I've never met a counterfeiter before," he said, tentatively.

"Yeah?" the man said. "Well, you'll never meet another like me, that's for sure. They don't make 'em like me any more."

"I know!" Pete said. "You're so good my friend wonders how you were ever caught."

"Just bad luck," Laurent said. He looked at Pete appraisingly.

"So why did you come back?" Pete asked. "I mean, why did you chance it?"

"To get what's mine," the man said. "We had a good thing going, me and the banker and the wine guy, for almost three years. It was foolproof. I printed the money and the banker gave me real money back. It was working great until the wine guy double-crossed me."

"What did he do?" Pete asked. He found he was genuinely interested. This was Jupiter's grandfather Laurent was talking about.

"He wanted to get away," Laurent said, "so he managed to print two million bucks without me knowing. He was going to run with the wife and kid. When I found out, my blood was boiling. I told him I'd kill his family if he didn't cough it up.

"No! the guy says. Don't hurt them! They don't know anything about it!

"Where is it? I asked him. In a wine barrel, he says. He was flailing his arms around, yelling, his face red as a beet.

"Wine barrel? I says. What wine barrel? Then he stopped flailing and he grabbed the front of his shirt and staggered toward me and toppled over, right on the floor. Heart attack. I never seen anything like it."

"Yikes!" Pete said.

"Tell me about it," Laurent said. "The place was full of wine barrels. Nothing *but* wine barrels. And the wife went to the Feds before I ever got a chance to find the money. I know where it is now, but it's not worth the risk. I spent enough time in jail. I'll just print some more money as soon as I get my hands on my plates."

This really *was* a bad guy – someone who would describe another person dying in such a cold and callous way. He determined to never tell Jupiter about Laurent's description of his grandfather's death.

If he ever got the chance to never tell Jupiter anything, he thought grimly.

At the sound of footsteps, Laurent swung the flashlight back up the cavern, and in its beam Pete could see Jupiter walking as fast as he could and carrying the case that held the engraved plates. Branko and Bob were close behind, their faces white in the glaring light.

They stopped as they approached. Laurent hauled Pete out from the wall and held him fast again, the knife against his throat. Did he have to do that? Pete wondered. With his other hand, Laurent swept the flashlight beam from Jupiter's feet to a spot beyond where Pete stood, indicating that they should move on by.

"No funny stuff," Laurent said. "I'm good with a knife."

"We've heard," Jupiter said. Sometimes, Pete thought, Jupiter should just stay quiet.

"And drop that right here," Laurent said.

Jupiter placed the case on the rock floor and walked past, followed by Branko and Bob.

"Are you O.K.?" Branko asked, looking worriedly at Pete.

"He's fine," Laurent said. "Now get moving."

When the boys were well past, Laurent took the knife away and hurriedly opened the case, removed the plates, and stuffed them in his own backpack. He was quick as a snake. In no time he had Pete again by the hands, with the knife blade against his throat.

"Hey," Pete said. "I thought we were – "

"Just because I talked to you," Laurent said, "doesn't mean I like you."

He turned toward Jupiter, Branko, and Bob and flashed his light in their faces. They all threw their hands up, squinting.

"Now. We're going to walk out of here. Very slowly. Just follow those red question marks," he said nastily.

Jupiter now looked stricken. As far as Pete could remember, this was the first time their question marks had actually helped a bad guy.

"I want the three of you to walk first,"

Laurent said, "in single file, so I can keep my eye on you. If any of you gets out of sight, if any of you makes a run for it, if any of you does anything that makes me think you're not doing exactly as I say, I'll stick this knife into your friend."

Jupiter nodded and turned toward the cave's exit. Branko and Bob followed. "Go on then," Laurent said, shoving Pete forward but keeping a firm hold on his tightly tied wrists.

Pete hoped the others had listened carefully and would do as Laurent had said. Because, as much as he didn't want to think about it, he knew this guy would carry through on his threat. He was, indeed, reckless, and reckless people did unpredictable things.

13

In Hot Pursuit

Bob shaded his eyes as they stumbled out of the cave into the glare of late morning sunlight. Jupiter walked slowly, so as not to get out of the counterfeiter's sight, and Branko and Bob followed. Behind him, Pete was talking to Laurent.

Bob was overwhelmed with admiration for his friend. When push came to shove, Pete always rose to the occasion. He snuck a glance over his shoulder from time to time. Pete's hands were tied behind his back, and his captor had a hold of him. But he'd put the knife away at least. Bob was very glad of that.

Pete looked calm – or as calm as anyone could look under the circumstances. His voice was steady and sounded much like it always did.

"But you won't need me," he was saying. "No way I can help you."

"That's where you're wrong, kid," Laurent said. "Hostages are worth their weight in gold. I'll dump you on the highway when I'm clear of this joint."

Oh, no! Bob thought. This was the first he'd heard of Laurent's plan. He wanted to cry out to Jupiter, but Laurent had said no talking. He thought he'd better follow orders. His stomach clenched and he found he was having a hard time getting a deep enough breath. His hands trembled.

He hated the idea of Pete being separated from him and Jupe, off on his own, in trouble. He remembered the case of the mysterious green ghost and the pearls that supposedly increased longevity. He and Jupiter had been held at the home of an old Chinese man, and when Pete had burst into the room they were being held in, Bob had been flooded with relief. Better they all be in trouble together than that one of them be in trouble by himself.

And they *were* all in trouble together, along with Branko. The five of them entered the vineyard proper and followed Jupiter down one of the long green aisles. In the distance the white of the farmhouse glimmered.

"Who's gonna be there?" Laurent asked. "And don't try to pull one over on me."

"No one's there," Pete said. "Branko's mom and dad are gone for the day, along with his brother and sister. The place is deserted."

"Is there a dog?" Laurent asked. "I

don't like dogs."

"He's just a puppy," Pete said. "Zeus wouldn't hurt a fly."

"There better be a car," Laurent was saying. "And it better work good."

"I told you," Pete said. "The Petrovics have a second car. A sedan. Mrs. Petrovic's car." Bob could hear it in Pete's voice – he was struggling with whether or not to tell Laurent about the Flex, and Pete's pride won out.

"We have our own car," Pete told Laurent. "But it's not here right now. Our friend Worthington took it away for the day."

Bob smiled. Not only was Pete proud of the car, but undeniably glad that the Flex was not available for André Laurent's plans.

"Worthington?" Laurent said. "What kind of sissy name is that?"

"It's a last name," Pete said. "And I can tell you for sure he's not a sissy." His voice had taken on an edge of something like anger. Watch it! Bob thought. Calm down.

But immediately Pete's voice grew conciliatory, even friendly. He knew what he was doing, Bob saw – trying to lull Laurent into a false sense of security.

"It's a really great car," Pete said. "You ever driven in a Flex? They're pretty rare."

"You crack me up, kid," Laurent said. "I don't know how much you know about prison, but they don't let you drive there."

"You can call me Pete," Pete said.

Laurent laughed. "Thanks, kid," he said.

Though Pete seemed to have things under control, Bob was very worried. He took a chance. "Jupe!" he whispered, hoping his voice would carry beyond Branko. Branko shot him a glance and then kept walking. He looked terrible, Bob thought. At least he and Pete and Jupe had been in danger before. This might be the first time for Branko.

"What is it?" Jupiter whispered, over his shoulder.

"He's going to try to take Pete hostage!" Bob said. "He's going to steal a car. We've got to get Pete away from this lunatic."

"Hey!" Laurent's voice cut through the morning air. "I said no talking!"

That shut Bob up.

As Jupiter emerged from the space between the grapevines, Branko and Bob quickly followed, and Bob heaved a great sigh of relief. It was good, at least, to be out in the open, with grass and space around.

Walking through the vineyard had felt claustrophobic, as though the vines were closing in — as though the vines were on Laurent's side. In no time they were standing in the gravel driveway in front of the Petrovic's house. The statue of the boy stood motionless, water constantly flowing from the jug in his hand. The only sound Bob could hear was the splashing of the fountain.

"O.K. Stop!" Laurent ordered. "Turn around."

Bob clustered together with Branko and Jupiter, and all three faced Pete. Laurent had taken his knife out of its sheath again.

"Which one of you lives here?" Laurent asked. Branko smiled meekly and signaled with his hand. "This is how it's going to be," Laurent said. "You go in the house and come back with the key to your mother's car."

In the distance, Bob heard the low drone of an automobile engine. He could see a rising plume of dust from what seemed to be the Petrovic's long driveway. Branko had just dashed into the house and was dashing out again, keys in hand, when Worthington pulled the Flex in, parked, and jumped out of the car, waving to the boys. But then he stopped, short, after taking in the scene before him.

"Hello, Worthington," Pete called in a cheerful voice. "You're back early."

Worthington clearly was at a loss for words and seemed to be wrestling with himself. Bob watched as the man's face changed rapidly, weighing his options. He decided the best thing to do was stay still for the moment.

"Hello, Pete," he said. "As it turned out, the man I went to see wasn't feeling very well. Who, may I ask, is your friend?"

"He's not my – !" Pete started.

"This is Mr. Laurent, Worthington," Jupiter said, stepping forward. "And he was just leaving."

"Yeah," Laurent said. "This car will do just fine. I mean, the kid here was telling me about how great it is and all, so thanks for bringing it back in time for me to take it. Just toss those keys over here. Right in the gravel, by the kid's feet."

Worthington did as he'd been told, and Laurent stooped and scooped up the keys in an instant.

"Now move out of the way. Go on, over there with the others." Worthington joined Jupiter and Bob, as Laurent pushed Pete roughly forward, toward the Flex.

He stopped before the back window and stared in disbelief at the decal, its iridescent edges shimmering in the sun. Bob could see it hadn't gotten dirty in the short time Worthington had been gone. The dragon, the lion, and the ram stared defiantly at André Laurent.

"What the hell's this?" he asked.

"It's a chimera," Pete said helpfully, "It's from Greek – "

"Shut up," Laurent said, "and get in the car."

He pulled Pete around, his hands still tied behind him, opened the passenger door, and shoved him in. Pete looked over his shoulder, out the window, searching for his friends. When he saw them, Bob could see his face relax.

"Don't worry," Pete called. "I'll be fine."

Laurent came around the back of the car. He walked toward Bob and the others, brandishing his knife, but stopped short of them.

"Well," he said. He smiled grimly. "Adios."

He hurried around and jumped into the driver's seat. The Flex's engine roared. Laurent jammed the car into reverse and sped backwards, almost hitting the fountain. He turned the wheel, stepped on the gas, and the Flex's wheels spun, spewing gravel. Then with the screech and smell of burning rubber, he took off up the Petrovics' driveway at top speed.

"Quick!" Jupiter yelled. "Everyone into the car! Give Worthington the keys, Branko!"

The four of them piled into Branko's mother's car — a 2012 Ford Focus sedan that had seen better days. It was an indeterminate color, somewhere between green and brown. Jupiter got into the front, next to Worthington, and Branko and Bob got into the back.

As soon as the engine roared, Bob and Branko both lowered their windows. The morning air, trapped in the car, had been heated by the sun, and sweat stood out on Bob's forehead almost instantly. Worthington jammed the sedan into reverse and backed up at such speed Bob felt himself been jerked forward.

"Bob, get out your cellphone and the GPS. Once we've caught up with Laurent, we'll call the police and use the GPS to update them on our location."

It felt good to be taking action, to be able to make decisions and operate freely again. He hadn't quite allowed himself to feel how terrible it was to be under the command and control of another person.

"Seatbelts!" Worthington ordered, as the car headed down the driveway. "A manual transmission!"

He shifted into second, fluidly working the clutch until he was up to top speed and they were roaring down the driveway, throwing gravel, in hot pursuit of the Flex. When they got to the driveway's end, Bob was unsure which way to turn, but Jupiter had been watching carefully, and he'd caught sight of the Flex just before it disappeared around a bend in the distance.

"That way," he said, pointing, and they were off.

The engine reached a high whining hum and stayed there. Bob felt himself being pressed back against the seat.

"Will Pete be O.K.?" Branko asked. In his lap were his two hands, one clenching the other. It was clear that he and Pete had become close. Bob remembered the two of them playing silly card games, getting up before Jupiter and him in the morning, tootling around the gift shop in search of suspicious personages.

"He'll be fine," Bob said. "It takes more than a homicidal maniac to keep Pete down."

Branko laughed, and Bob realized he was making a joke to defuse his own worries. As much to reassure himself as to reassure

Branko, he said, "He's been in a couple close calls in the past, but he's come out of them without a scratch."

"Well," Jupiter said. "I wouldn't go that far. He's had a couple of bruises and a couple of scrapes – but then we all have."

"Yes," Worthington said. "And let us remember that though Pete might cower before a mouse, he will stand steadfast in front of a lion."

He was driving as fast as he safely could – which was surprisingly fast. There were no other cars on the road so he was straddling the center line, staying safely away from the edges where the old asphalt crumbled into gravel. Bob could see the Flex growing slowly larger in the windshield. It turned a corner up ahead and Bob took note.

"Do you think Laurent knows where he's going?" Branko asked.

"Turn here," Bob said when they reached the spot where the Flex had turned. Worthington jerked the wheel and the Ford rose briefly up on two wheels.

"I expect so," Jupiter said calmly. "Remember he lived here for years, and the roads haven't changed. But I don't think he has a destination other than Away."

"My guess," Worthington said, "is that he'll stay far from the Interstate, and even the major highways, if he can. He'll try to keep to back roads where it'll be harder to find him. Hold on."

They went around a curve at top speed, the back tires skidding to the right. Bob's heart was pounding, but he trusted Worthington, who looked totally calm and collected – even more calm than Pete had looked.

They were approaching the outskirts of Jackson now, and there were more houses dotting the landscape. Bob was worried that the increased density of population would mean more cars and the possibility of losing Laurent. But Worthington had him firmly in his sights.

"It's time to call 911," Worthington said.

"Yes," Jupiter said. "I agree. Give the phone to me, Bob. You check our progress on the GPS and I'll relay it to the police."

Jupiter dialed 911 and Bob zeroed in on the GPS. When the dispatcher answered, Jupiter quickly told her the story.

"Armed and dangerous," he said. "He's driving a gray Ford Flex with a black top. He's got one of our friends with him as a hostage. We're close behind him in another car."

Worthington veered onto Hopkins Road.

"Where are we?" Jupiter asked Bob. "Hopkins Road," Bob said, "heading northeast." Jupiter relayed the information and explained about the GPS. He covered the receiver.

"They're in their cruisers," he said. "They'll set up a roadblock."

"Roger that," Bob said. He kept his eyes glued to the GPS, following the little blinking dot as the car rocketed around curves and whizzed around corners. Each time Worthington turned, Bob barked out the name of the new road and the direction of travel and Jupiter relayed it to the 911 dispatcher.

"Old Creek Road," he told her. "Hoffer Street. He's turning north on State Route 3."

The old state route was narrow and relatively straight. They crested a hill and saw, about a hundred yards ahead, two black-and-white cruisers pulled across the highway. Six policemen stood with their pistols drawn in fighting stance. The Flex screeched to a halt and Laurent tried to back up and turn, but another cruiser came careening from the side and blocked his retreat.

Worthington pulled the sedan over and all four of them hurriedly got out, in time to watch Laurent ease from the car with his hands up.

"Let me out!" Pete yelled. Bob rushed to the passenger side of the Flex and untied Pete's wrists. "Thanks!" Pete said. "My hands went to sleep." He stood there rubbing his wrists.

As the police were handcuffing Laurent, the four boys hurried up to him. Seen now, in police custody, he didn't look so threatening, Bob thought.

"Hello, Mr. Laurent," Jupiter said.

Laurent scowled at them in fury.

"The Three Investigators!" he said.

"And Branko Petrovic!" Pete said loyally.

"These boys were courageous and determined," the policeman said. "They were more than a match for you."

"Never underestimate your adversaries," Jupiter said. "Although I really *was* very stupid for taking my friends into danger in the cave in the first place. I should have realized that you might also be there."

"Too bad you didn't, kid," Laurent said. "Really, really too bad."

The policeman put his hand on Laurent's head and pushed him into the back seat of the cruiser as the boys walked away to talk privately.

"Wow!" Pete said. "That was something! Luckily he didn't hurt the Flex."

Branko rushed up and hugged Pete.

"My friend!" he said. "You are all right? Bob and Jupiter told me you would be."

"Yeah," Pete said. "I guess I am. Remind me never to go in another cave! But while Laurent and I were waiting for the three of you to get back with the plates, at least he told me the last piece of the story. He said that Spiridon Markovic managed to print two million dollars in counterfeit money — that he was going to use it to run, with your mother and grandmother.

"When Laurent found out, he told Spiridon he'd kill his family if he didn't hand it over. Your grandfather had a heart attack before he could. But Laurent told me Spiridon Markovic had put the money in a barrel."

"That's all very important information," Jupiter said. "I think we should involve the police in the recovery of the barrel."

Shortly afterwards, Jupiter was conferring with a policeman and policewoman. When he was finished, he came over to say that one of the cops would return Mrs. Petrovic's car to Cornucopia, another would take Laurent to the lock-up, and Worthington would drive the Flex with the four boys in it — following a black-and-white that would lead the way to Dragutin, so they could all talk to Michael Ivan.

Pete sat in the front in his customary position, rubbing his wrists. Bob could see they were raw and red. Jupiter had been right; Pete had had plenty of scrapes. But he really seemed none the worse for wear.

"We got him!" he said, "I knew we would. I just didn't know when!"

"Yes," Jupiter said. "It seems we've come to a successful conclusion to both our cases. Though I have to say it was touch-and-go there for a while."

It took longer than Bob had imagined it would to get back to the road on which Dragutin Wines was located. Laurent had led them on quite a chase. Also, the policeman driving the cruiser was in no hurry – probably basking in the success of the capture, Bob thought. Though he didn't put his siren on, he flashed the blue-and-red lights atop the car. Bob had never had a police escort before.

"You were brave," Branko said to Pete.

"You certainly were," Jupiter said. "As always."

"Laurent isn't such a bad guy when you get to know him," Pete said.

"Yeah, right," Bob said. "Like his friend Genghis Khan."

"At least he didn't hurt the Flex!" Pete said. "I was more worried about the car than I was about me. I kept worrying he'd crash it into something."

"With you inside," Bob said.

"I was just worried about the car," said Pete.

When they got to Dragutin Wines, the policeman pulled up next to the winery's office, and Michael Ivan came out in a hurry, looking worried.

"Hello, officer," he said. "We were just cleaning up after last night's fireworks. Is something the matter?"

"We've just arrested André Laurent," the policeman said. "This time he won't be getting bail."

A look of immense relief crossed Michael Ivan's face. Bob supposed he'd known Laurent was around and was glad to hear he wouldn't be showing up anytime soon.

Bob and the others came over to where Ivan was standing. "This young man has a favor to ask," the policeman said, gesturing to Jupiter, "and I think you should grant it."

"Hello, Mr. Ivan," Jupiter said. "We're here a day earlier than expected, but it couldn't be helped." He briefly explained what they were there for.

The gift shop was closed for the day, but Michael Ivan led the long parade of boys and police and Worthington to the door, unlocked it, and turned off the alarm. He flicked a few switches and the whole place was flooded with light.

"This way," he said.

Even though Bob knew what they were going to do, he was quite excited. In the museum section of the shop, they all crowded around the wine barrel with the stenciling – DRAGUTIN WINES and SPIRIDON MARCOVIC and 1995.

"Spiridon Marcovic was my grandfather," Jupiter said in a cool, explanatory tone, "forced into criminal activity to save his family and his livelihood. But he wanted out. This money was his escape plan."

Bob watched in mounting excitement next to Pete, who had a massive grin on his face. Jupiter handed Michael Ivan his Swiss Army knife, and with its largest blade, Ivan slit the red wax seal all the way around the barrel. The wax was thick and it took a while. Ivan wound up having to gouge some of the wax away so he could get at the lid.

He pried the top up and wrenched it off.

Even empty, an oak wine barrel like this one must weigh over a hundred pounds, Bob thought, and as he and the others peered inside, they could see that it wasn't empty at all. At the bottom, it actually held the dried and husky remnants of something that might have been a grapevine, but on top of the rubble sat packets and packets – and packets and *packets* – of apparently perfect one-hundred-dollar bills. Michael Ivan gasped in astonishment, then picked up a packet and examined it carefully.

Finally, he said, "I haven't seen money like this for twenty-five years. Money that looks like the real thing, but that I know for certain isn't."

Jupiter turned to the policeman who'd led the way. "I think you should call the federal authorities," he said. "The F.B.I. at least, and maybe the Secret Service. The Secret Service, after all, takes care of counterfeiting cases, unless I'm mistaken."

"We'll have to take the barrel," the policeman told Mr. Ivan, "as evidence."

"Of course," Michael Ivan said. "But, with its contents, it weighs over a hundred and fifty pounds."

"Maybe we can lighten the load a little by taking a couple of packets as a souvenir,"

Bob joked.

One of the cops said they'd need to call for back-up in order to get the barrel loaded in a secure vehicle; in the meantime, another cop wrote down the names and addresses of all the boys in his notebook. He told Pete he would probably have to testify in court.

"Really?" Pete said, surprised.

"Well, he abducted you," the policeman said. "If we charge him with abduction, you'll have to testify. When can the five of you come down to the station to file a formal report?"

"We'll have to come tomorrow," Jupiter said. "We're busy for the rest of the day."

"Yes," Branko said. "We first have to conclude another case we've solved. A missing persons case." He pointed to Jupiter. "And he's the missing person."

Jupiter, Bob, and Pete all laughed. The policeman looked puzzled but didn't pursue it. Bob thought that had been clever of Branko – though from *their* point of view, it had been Jupiter's mother's family that had been missing. Still, from the point of view of the Pelletiers it had been Jupiter, and tonight he'd be with them again.

Bob remembered the evening before, when he and Jupe had been cleaning up after the cookout, and he'd caught Jupiter looking out the window at the Petrovics with an inscrutable look on his face. Of course, Jupiter had always had his aunt and uncle, who loved him very much. But there were only two of them, and they were old enough to be his grandparents. They were also very different from Jupiter in a lot of important ways. Everyone wanted a family to belong to, Bob thought.

At long last, Jupiter Jones had one.

14

A Good Place For Nessie

Two days later, Mallory MacLeod was back at work at the Jones Salvage Yard. It was a hot sunny afternoon in southern California, with a slight breeze wafting over the fence, and Mallory was in the shade, busy with old picture frames.

There were, literally, hundreds that Titus Jones had scrounged, bought, and bartered for over the years, of all shapes and sizes, and sorting the good from the bad, the salable from the throw-awayable was a multi-day project. Mallory was bundling most of them into multi-frame lots.

Nevertheless, she was there that afternoon not because she was fond of picture frames, or even because she liked her job − though she definitely did − but because The Three Investigators were due back from Jackson, and Mallory was intent on being there to welcome them home.

The afternoon before, Uncle Titus had been sitting in the Salvage Yard's office, leafing through an issue of *Bargain Hunters* while Mal-

lory was typing the beginning of her picture
frame inventory into the business's computer.
The phone rang. Aunt Mathilda picked up.

"Oh, hello, Jupiter," she said.

Mallory watched as her face changed
into a mask of astonishment and her mouth fell
open into a perfect "O."

"Land sakes!" Aunt Mathilda said in a
voice equal parts incredulity and glee. "Two
million counterfeit dollars!"

That certainly got Titus Jones's attention.

"Let me put you on speakerphone!" said
Aunt Mathilda. "Your uncle and Mallory are
both here with me in the office."

She punched the speakerphone button
and Mallory heard the familiar echoing hum of
ambient noise.

"Hello, Jupiter?" Aunt Mathilda said.
"Are you still there?"

After a moment, Jupiter cleared his
throat. "Yes, I am," he said. "I wasn't expecting a crowd."

"Well, it's not a crowd," Aunt Mathilda
said. "It's just us."

"Hello, Uncle Titus," Jupiter said.
"Hello, Mallory."

"Two million counterfeit dollars?" Uncle

Titus said.

"There's no need to go into detail right now," Jupiter said. "There'll be plenty of time for us to tell you the whole story when we're back in Rocky Beach. Worthington is driving us back tomorrow. I expect we'll arrive mid-afternoon, say 3 or 3:30."

"That's fine and dandy," Aunt Mathilda said. "But at least tell them what you told me so I know I was hearing you right."

Jupiter cleared his throat again. Clearly this was making him uncomfortable. He'd called to let his aunt know when to expect him, not to give a speech, Mallory thought.

"As I said, Pete, Bob, and I helped in the arrest of an ex-convict named André Laurent — a counterfeiter who returned to the scene of the crime to recover two million dollars in counterfeit currency. Unfortunately for him, we recovered it instead. We've just returned from making a full report to the authorities."

"What authorities?" Uncle Titus asked.

"The F.B.I. and the Secret Service," Jupiter said.

This impressed Uncle Titus beyond words, Mallory could see. His nephew and the Secret Service!

"You don't say!" Uncle Titus murmured

in a hushed and reverent voice.

"They were very grateful," Jupiter said.

"And impressed, I'll bet!" Aunt Mathilda said proudly.

"They were not *un*impressed," Jupiter said mildly.

From the conversation that followed, Mallory had learned that Jupiter, Bob, Pete, and Branko had taken both the authorities and the landowners to a cave that connected Cornucopia Wines with a neighboring vineyard and shown them the secret cavern workshop where the counterfeiting had been done.

The agents had been, as Jupiter had put it, "marginally embarrassed" that their predecessors had failed to discover the counterfeiter's lair twenty-five years earlier, when the crime had been committed.

"We consoled them," Jupiter said, "as best we could."

"What happened to the two million counterfeit dollars?" Uncle Titus asked.

"The police surrendered it to the Secret Service," Jupiter said. "Together with the barrel it had come in."

The word "surrendered" made Mallory smile. She had an image of two million fake dollars with their hands up.

"The barrel?" Uncle Titus asked. "What barrel?"

"I really can't talk any more right now," Jupiter had said, his voice taking on an edge of exasperation. "Since I have something else to tell you, I'll call you at the house tonight."

He had, and today when Mallory had come in, the first thing Aunt Mathilda had done was to tell her what Jupiter had wanted to keep private. Astonishingly enough, while he and the others had been staying at Cornucopia Wines, running into this man André Laurent, Jupiter had also managed to run into a long-lost branch of his mother's family.

"Land sakes!" Aunt Mathilda kept saying. "It seems he met his grandmother's sister! And his mother's first cousin! And two second cousins who are twins! Twins! I ask you!"

"Boys or girls?" Mallory asked.

"A boy *and* a girl," Aunt Mathilda said, triumphantly. "They're eleven years old, Jupiter says!"

A boy *and* a girl, Mallory thought, a little jealous, somehow. No, really, this wasn't jealousy she was feeling, she realized; it was a strange sort of admiration for Jupiter – who, in less than a week, had gone from having no cousins of any kind at all to having a perfectly matched set.

It was now several hours later; when Mallory looked at her watch, it said 2:35, and since the boys were due at 3:00, she was beginning to get excited. The Three Investigators as a rule were pretty punctual, and she had to admit that she was very much looking forward to seeing them. In fact, she'd missed them. They'd been gone for almost six days, and that was the longest period of time Mallory had gone without seeing at least one or the other of them since she'd met them a month ago.

Soon they'd be back, Worthington at the wheel, and if things had gone slightly differently, she'd be with them. Ever since Jupiter had invited her up to Jackson for the Fourth, she'd pondered what the invitation meant. It had come so out of the blue — from the one member of the trio who had been most cautious with her — that she had to interpret it as a good sign.

In a way, she thought, it was fortuitous that she'd had to say no. Jupiter's invitation was last minute — though no less welcome for that — and she'd had a real excuse because of the commitment she'd made to her mother. She'd gotten the benefit of feeling great about having been invited without any of the danger of things having gone awry if she'd actually gone up to Jackson.

After all, the boys were so used to operating as a threesome that they'd undoubtedly had to make accommodations to include Branko Petrovic, and if she'd been there, it would have complicated things beyond endurance. She was sure that, in retrospect, Jupiter was relieved she'd said no. He might even feel obscurely grateful to her.

She'd done well in the "Kit Carson case," as Uncle Titus had dubbed it, when she'd gotten a copy of the forged letter from Daniel Hernández. But now that she knew what Jupiter, Pete, and Bob had faced up in Jackson – well, Daniel Hernández, a vainglorious university professor with a nefarious scheme, was one thing, and a murdering thieving counterfeiter with a hunting knife was something else entirely.

Aunt Mathilda and Uncle Titus came over to where she was sorting the picture frames. They were both in a jocular mood.

"The boys should be back any time now," Aunt Mathilda said. Her face was rosy with anticipation. Clearly, she'd missed Jupiter, too. "How are you doing with those frames, sweetie?"

"Pretty well, thank you," Mallory said. "There sure are a lot of them, Mr. Jones."

Titus Jones looked at her brightly. "Yes, my dear," he said. "I suppose there are. I never could resist a picture frame. You never know when one will come in handy."

Mallory supposed he might be right, though she doubted it. She hoped that by bundling ten or fifteen of them together, she might be able to find buyers for something that otherwise would end up in a rubbish bin.

"I was just saying to Mathilda," Uncle Titus said. "Jupiter told me that, since the summer began, he and the boys have been keeping mementos of their cases. They came back from the Gold Country with an assayer's scale, but all they got from their Kit Carson case was two books signed by their authors. With this case, I was hoping they'd get to keep the money they discovered."

"But it's just a lot of paper!" Aunt Mathilda said. "It's counterfeit! You can't spend it."

"I could try," Uncle Titus said, winking.

"Come on, Titus," Aunt Mathilda said. "We're going to the office to rest our old bones and wait for Jupiter."

"I'll be here if you need me," Mallory said, turning back to her bundling.

However, Uncle Titus's mention of The Three Investigators' mementos reminded Mallory that CALIFORNIA, CORNUCOPIA OF THE WORLD still leaned against the office's back wall where she'd left it. After she'd found it and decided to buy it, she'd thought of giving it to the boys as a present – but just because of the coincidence of them visiting Branko at Cornucopia Wines.

Now it seemed as if it might be a fitting reminder of their most recent case. A kind of joke, sort of – about a place where not only peaches, oranges, grapes, plums, and a pineapple spilled in endless profusion from the horn of plenty, but so did money. She thought they'd like the joke; maybe she'd give them the print later today.

Of course, in her *own* mind, Mallory thought, the print had become associated with something slightly different – the fact that although people wanted things to stay the way they always had been, they never, ever did. There was no such thing as a certainty in this life – except, perhaps, as the old saying went, death and taxes.

Mallory picked up several bundles of frames and was leaning them against the tall wooden fence that surrounded the Salvage

Yard when she heard the crunch of gravel and turned to see the Flex coming through the wrought-iron gate. She hurriedly put down the frames. She had the impulse to run, but she checked herself, not wanting to seem overeager.

Aunt Mathilda and Uncle Titus came out of the office at the same time, so there was quite a welcoming committee as the boys clambered out of their car. While Mr. and Mrs. Jones talked to Worthington, Mallory approached the boys, suddenly feeling shy.

Though it had been less than a week since she'd seen them, it seemed to her almost as if she were seeing them for the first time. All three had obviously spent a lot of time in the sun. Pete was tan and powerfully built and even better-looking than she remembered. His easy athleticism was translated into his graceful physical presence. His brown eyes glittered with energy and good humor.

"Mallory!" he cried.

Bob waved to her, grinning. In the afternoon sun his blondish hair seemed lit from within. He looked a little burned, actually, and a little tired. He was clearly glad to see her – though he was less forthcoming than Pete. He was, after all, more restrained in general –

though, in a way, as Records and Research, he was the foundation of The Three Investigators, Mallory reflected.

Of the three, Jupiter seemed the most different. Could he have grown taller in a week? She'd heard that could happen at this age. It was not as though he'd been transformed so much as that he'd become even more himself. His green-blue eyes gleamed with intelligence; he looked ready to take on all comers. He'd been briefly flustered when she'd talked to him on the phone, but that fluster was gone now. Given all that had happened, she wasn't surprised that he'd regained his sense of authority and command.

Everyone was saying hello to everyone else when Leif and Magnus joined them.

"It's been quiet around here since you left," Leif said to Jupiter. "Nice and peaceful."

"Too quiet," Magnus said. "Welcome back."

The tale of everything that had happened tumbled forth in bits and pieces as each of the boys chimed in – though Jupiter held the master narrative, filling in or explaining where necessary. But he let Pete tell the story of being held at knifepoint all by himself, without any interruptions, and Mallory had to say she was very impressed. Pete could be a bit over-enthusiastic sometimes, but he had real grit and real guts.

She could see the boys were beginning to flag, so Mallory wasn't surprised when Worthington helped Jupiter unload his luggage and his bike, then suggested that maybe he should take Pete and Bob home.

"Wait a minute, Worthington," Bob said. "We had no idea that Mallory would be here when we got back, but since she is, I think that now might be a good time to show her Leif and Magnus's recent project."

"Their project?" Mallory said. "You mean the project Leif asked me to tell Jupiter was finished?"

"Yes," said Bob. "That project." He turned to Jupiter and Pete. "What do you say?" he asked.

Jupiter nodded and Pete said, "Let's do it!" Mallory was mystified, but followed the boys and Worthington – who, in turn, were following Leif and Magnus. As they walked, Aunt Mathilda moved beside her and squeezed Mallory's shoulder hard. Although Mallory generally didn't like to be touched all that much, by now she was almost used to Aunt Mathilda's habit, and, in this case, the quality of her shoulder squeeze seemed to communicate that something nice was about to happen – presumably to Mallory, though, unfortunately, in front of an audience.

The nine of them reached Leif and Magnus's workshop, and as soon as she got inside, Mallory saw a large rectangular shape, covered by a tarp.

"Bob," Jupiter said, "you do the honors. After all, this was your idea."

Bob grabbed a corner of the tarp and yanked it off. The assembled company oohed and aahed while Mallory stared and stared.

She was looking at a rectangular trunk made of oak, varnished and lustrous in the afternoon light, and raised off the ground on semi-flattened large bun feet. The trunk had gorgeous wrought-iron handles on either end, and as she slowly walked around it, she saw that it also had wrought-iron strapping on the rough wooden back – which, to her joy, wasn't varnished or lustrous, but unfinished, just the way a reproduction should be.

By now, Mallory had realized that it *was* a reproduction – and a reproduction of a very specific trunk. The first time she'd seen The Three Investigators together, they'd been in a bookstore in Grass Valley which had had a trunk very much like this one – an immigrant's trunk marked with the owner's name, and the date of her arrival in America.

On the front of that one – as on the front of this – there'd been an elaborate iron lock with a gigantic metal key. Mallory remembered the original trunk perfectly, and as she looked at this one, she saw that the size of its banded top – which overhung its sides – was once again matched by intricate molding at the bottom, so that it was perfectly symmetrical.

As for the front, it had three inset wooden panels, and although the lock and key were at the top of the central panel, underneath them was painted not 1845, but the date of the current year.

After Leif and Magnus had built it, the trunk had been decorated by an artist of exquisite taste, and the left inset panel was painted with the name *Mallory MacLeod* in an elegant script, while the right had a pedestal holding painted flowers. On each end, the wrought-iron handle was set in the center of a painted and mitered box also holding flowers, and on the top were two more painted boxes with flowers inside them and garlands around them.

Tears came to Mallory's eyes but she blinked them back. The trunk would have been incredible enough, she thought, but the fact that one (or all) of the boys had noticed her admiring the original at the Next Chapter Bookstore and decided to have one like it made for her was almost beyond belief. Her very own immigrant's trunk, she thought – marked with her name and the date of her arrival in the United States.

Remembering what Jupiter had said a little while before, Mallory said to Bob, "*You* thought of this?"

"I saw you looking at the one in Grass Valley and took some pictures with my cellphone," Bob confessed.

"Leif and Magnus had two designs," Pete interjected excitedly. "This one, with a flat top, and another with a domed lid. You know, one that rose in the middle. Would you have liked that one better? We wanted to give you something you really liked!"

"I love this one. I adore it, actually," Mallory said. "Not only is it *exactly* like the one we saw in the bookstore, but it's also more practical than a trunk with a domed lid. I can use it as a table or a bench as well as to keep stuff in."

"Bob thought that was how you'd feel," Jupiter said.

After that, there was a lot of excited chatter, and Leif and Magnus demonstrated how the lock worked. To Mallory's additional pleasure and amazement, when Leif turned the key and lifted the lid, she saw that there was a wooden tray that could be lifted in and out by its cut-out wooden handles.

She was really overwhelmed, and after thanking all three boys (as well as Leif and Magnus) several times, she found herself saying, "I have something for you, too. It's nothing like *this*, of course, but I think you might like it."

She turned and dashed out of the workshop, across the gravel, to the building in which she'd stored the framed print. Ripping the SOLD sticker off the corner, she dashed back to the workshop and ran in, holding the print behind her for a moment. Pete kept trying to sneak a look.

"It's just something I found here at the Salvage Yard, but it made me think of you guys when you were up at Cornucopia."

She brought the print from behind her and held it in front.

"Wow!" Pete said. "It's beautiful! California! Cornucopia of the world!"

"What a fantastic historical artifact,"

Bob said. "You could write a whole article about it. A whole book."

"This is not only thoughtful of you, Mallory," Jupiter said, "but remarkably *apropos*."

"If you don't have another memento of your recent case," Mallory said, "maybe you'll consider this one."

"We don't have to consider it," said Jupiter. "We'll hang it on the wall of Headquarters the next time we're in it."

"Of course," Uncle Titus said, "counterfeit money would have been better – more in keeping with the case, don't you think?" He winked at Mathilda.

"Perhaps for one of the cases we solved," Jupiter said, "but not for the other. Counterfeit money has nothing to do with that."

"You mean the second cousins who are twins!" Aunt Mathilda chortled. "Twins! I ask you!"

After that, there was a lot of thanking. Mallory again thanked everyone for the part, small or large, that they'd played in the gift of the immigrant's trunk. The boys thanked her for the poster. Jupiter thanked Worthington for the estimable part he'd played in the adventure,

286

and soon they were moving Pete's and Bob's gear to the side in the back of the Flex in order to fit in Mallory's trunk and deliver it to her house for her.

Worthington also fastened her bike to the bike rack – after which Jupiter stood with his aunt and uncle, waving, as Worthington took off with Pete in the passenger's seat and Bob and Mallory in the back.

As Mallory had clambered in, she'd noticed that the back of the Flex had dark tinted windows, and as she fastened her seat belt, she wondered whether she would be visible or invisible to anyone looking in. Invisible, she decided, and as Worthington drove the short distance from the Salvage Yard to the Wessex House, she sat back in her seat and listened to Pete tell the story of how Jupiter had discovered his great-aunt, his second cousins, and his first cousin once removed just as the Fourth of July fireworks came to an end at Dragutin Wines.

However, even as she listened, she was thinking about the boy who was sitting quietly beside her – the boy who had somehow figured out what kind of gift she might like and who had also imagined how she might want to use it, once she had it. Bob was really a special boy, she thought.

Just then, Worthington turned into the street where the Wessex House was located, and to her real dismay – and even horror – Mallory saw her own first cousin, Skinny Norris, parked in his sports car on the street.

His car was running, but the window was rolled all the way down, and Skinny had his hand out, jerking it in time to inaudible music.

"Oh, no," she groaned, interrupting Pete in mid-story. "Look who's here, for some god-awful reason. And I was just feeling so happy. I wish Skinny would lose my address. Permanently."

Without planning to, Mallory found herself unbuckling her seat belt and scrunching down as far as she could in the back seat. She saw Worthington observing this in the rear view mirror, and then, to her surprise, she saw him simply pass Skinny's car and proceed to the end of the block, where he turned right at the corner. There, he stopped the car.

"So that's the infamous Skinny Norris?" he asked. "If I ever met him, I don't remember, and I don't think he's ever seen the Flex. I'm a pretty good actor, if I do say so myself, and I'm thinking that maybe I'll just stroll back and tell Skinny I own the Wessex House and that it's time for him to get lost."

"Oh, Worthington, would you?" asked Mallory in something like awe. "That would be brilliant. From one ex-pat to another," she added. *"Brilliant."*

Though she was sure her remark sounded like garbled nonsense to Bob and Pete, she could see that Worthington had understood her.

"It's time these boys learned some good British slang," he said. "And I'll be happy to send that wanker packing."

He climbed out of the car and strode around the corner. In very short order, Skinny's red sports car drove away – fast – from where he had been parked. When Worthington returned, he drove the Flex around the block, eased it into the driveway of the Wessex House, then unloaded Mallory's bike from the bike rack.

Mallory hugged him. "Thank you, Worthington," she said. "I can't believe you got rid of him!"

"Just call Worthington's Pest Control," he said cheerily.

While Worthington and Mallory walked in front, Pete and Bob each took one of the wrought-iron handles of Mallory's trunk and carried it through the front door and down the narrow hall, careful not to bump it.

Mallory's mother wasn't home yet, so Mallory opened the apartment door with her key. Then – with Worthington at her side – she led the way into her bedroom. Luckily, the room was neat and tidy, and Mallory only had to move a single wooden chair to make room for the trunk under the comfortably rattly Victorian windows.

"Would you put it here?" she asked Bob and Pete.

They did as she had asked, then turned to her, beaming.

"It looks great!" Pete said.

"I'll say," Bob said.

"A fine placement of a fine piece," said Worthington approvingly. "Well, I'd best get these boys back to their homes in time for dinner," he added.

Mallory followed them back outside.

"Thanks again," she said to Bob and Pete. "Really. I'm going to treasure that trunk forever."

She waved them all the way down the street, until they were out of sight.

Back in her room, alone with The Three Investigators' thank-you gift, Mallory really allowed herself to feel its full import. Sure, she'd helped Pete and Bob and Jupiter with their case up in Auburn – but only by accident, and it would have been easy for them to thank her with a box of chocolates or a bunch of flowers. They hadn't done that.

Mallory turned the key and opened the trunk to peer inside it, then closed the lid and studied the lovely twining vines of flowers which wove around its lid. After a minute she took her shoes off and lay down on the trunk with her knees up and her hands behind her head. Then she swung her feet down again and slid to the floor, so that she could sit and scrutinize her painted name and the year of her arrival in the United States.

As she ran her finger over the subtle colors, she remembered saying to Worthington, "From one ex-pat to another."

Why had she called herself an ex-pat? she wondered suddenly. Well, he had used the term first, several days ago. Nevertheless, immigrant trunk or no immigrant trunk, she wasn't *that* – not yet, at least. She had two more years to decide whether or not she actually wanted to stay in the United States – and although, in general, Mallory liked to make her mind up fairly quickly, in *this* case, she intended to take all of the remaining seven hundred days to see how things panned out in Rocky Beach.

Impulsively, she jumped back to her feet. From her bedside table she took the rubber replica of the Loch Ness monster she'd won as a prize at the Scottish music camp the day before she'd met The Three Investigators at the Next Chapter Bookstore and set it on the trunk lid where it stood proudly, its long green snaky neck reaching for the ceiling.

When she'd first won it, Mallory had thought it a little silly, but since then she'd become very fond of it. She looked at its green rubber feet planted firmly on one of the lid's painted flowers and said, "Don't worry, Nessie. I won't be any easier to catch than you are!"

She found herself wondering if that was really true. Probably not, she thought. In fact, she was probably caught already.

15

A Chimeric Cornucopia

It was two days later, and while Jupiter wasn't thinking about Mallory right at the moment, he'd been thinking about her quite a bit, on and off, for the last two days. There'd been something about the unexpected and almost magical realization he'd had at the Fourth of July celebration that had taken his life and shaken it up. The people sitting next to him on the blanket, watching the fireworks explode overhead, weren't just friends of the Petrovics', but his own great-aunt, a first cousin once removed, and two second cousins.

He had liked all of the members of the Pelletier family even before he knew they were *his* family, but he'd had an oddly intense feeling for Harper, and now he knew why. Because she was like a younger — and female — version of himself — and somewhere in the strands of his Welsh/Serbian DNA, there were some strands that matched some of Harper's to a T.

The thing was, all his life, Jupiter had felt that feelings, while undeniably powerful and interesting, were not really a reliable guide to proper actions, and although he still felt that, he knew that if he'd tried to make a list of all the feelings he'd had between the time The Three Investigators had arrived at Cornucopia Wines and the time they had left, it would have been quite long. And every feeling had had its flipside. As exhilarating as it had been to discover his mother's aunt and her son and grandchildren living right there in Jackson, California – and as nice as it was to have new friends in the Petrovics – it was frustrating to think that they all lived so far away.

It was a long, long drive to Jackson, and even with a car of their own, and a driver willing to take them wherever they wanted to go, the trip to Jackson was one he and his friends couldn't take all that often if they wanted to keep working cases. And they did. It was therefore surprisingly comforting to know that their other new friend, Mallory MacLeod, not only lived right in Rocky Beach but that she worked right in the Salvage Yard, where Jupiter and the others could see her often.

The strange thing was that when Bob had suddenly suggested they give her the immigrant's chest the moment they got back, Jupiter had been surprised by how intensely he'd hoped she would like it – for her sake, but also for

Bob's, since he knew that Bob liked her quite a lot. In fact, he could see that Bob had developed a real crush. Still, the thing that would really stick with him from the moment when Bob grabbed a corner of the tarp and yanked it off the chest was the clarity with which Mallory had showed she liked not just the general idea, but every single detail of the chest.

Unless Jupiter's eyes had deceived him, she had almost started crying. And since she clearly wasn't someone who cried all that often – and probably never in public, if she could help it! – that had really meant something.

As for Jupiter, although he wasn't normally given to feelings of general gratitude about his life, he had to admit that he couldn't remember a time when he had ever felt quite so grateful for the people around him. Right now, he was sitting at the desk in Headquarters, waiting for Pete and Bob to arrive – and *not* for a debriefing about the case.

Normally, at the end of a Three Investigators mystery, there were lots of loose ends to be tied up, but this time, there really didn't seem to be any. At least, not technical ones. Of course, at some point in the future he and Pete and Bob would be asked to testify at André Laurent's trial, and one of the men from the

Secret Service had mentioned that they would be asking Jupiter, Pete, and Bob to sign some sort of form.

But today they were meeting because when the three of them had been driving back from Jackson, Pete had told Bob and Jupiter that he'd had a terrific idea he wanted to share – and today was the day he was going to share it. While Pete frequently had what Jupiter considered terrific ideas, he couldn't remember another occasion when Pete had wanted to call a special meeting to discuss one. He wondered what it was.

As he sat, he opened his own special drawer in the firm's desk. This drawer wasn't locked, but in it, Jupiter kept special items he wanted to consider further. Right now, on the very top, lay the piece of heavy paper with his right footprint impressed on it in ink together with an envelope embossed with the name and address of John Pelletier's consulting firm.

The day he and his friends had gone to the Pelletiers for dinner, John Pelletier had taken Jupiter aside before they left, laughing conspiratorially as he handed Jupiter the envelope.

"I wouldn't stay in business long if I kept putting bills like these in envelopes," he'd said.

Inside, Jupiter had found the five counterfeit hundred-dollar bills which had been hidden in André Laurent's leather satchel, under the false bottom.

"I thought you might like these," John Pelletier had said, smiling, "to remind you of how you discovered your missing family."

Jupiter had been genuinely touched at the gesture, and, today, he was just taking the bills out of the envelope and arranging them on the desk when first Bob and then Pete came in through Easy Three.

"Whoa!" Pete said. "Are those what I think they are?"

"If you think they're the counterfeit bills that were hidden in André Laurent's satchel, then yes," Jupiter said. "John Pelletier gave them to me just before we left his house, the night we went to dinner there. I've examined them several times now, and I can find no deviation whatever between them and normal bills. Of course, I'm no expert, but I still think they're an impressive piece of work."

"I didn't see Mr. Pelletier give them to you!" Pete said.

"Why would you have?" Bob asked. "You were off in the corner talking to Connor O'Malley. How wild that he was in Jackson for his 4-H mentoring the same night we went to dinner at the Pelletiers.”

“I really like him,” Pete said. “But that wasn’t why I was talking with him.”

“Really?” Bob asked. “Why were you talking with him, then?”

“I was asking him to do something for me. Well, for all of us, really. As an artist.”

Pete paused and looked uncertain about how to proceed.

“When we first started The Three Investigators, Jupiter thought of using three question marks as our trademark, and “We Investigate Anything” as our motto, and when we got our website Bob had the great idea of making his case titles alphabetical. Well, I’ve had an idea, too,” he said.

He paused again, still looking a little nervous, Jupiter thought – worried that his idea wouldn’t meet with his friends’ approval.

“Are you going to tell us,” Jupiter asked him, “or just keep us in suspense?”

“Remember when we first saw the Ford Flex?” Pete said. “And I said the chimera on the back sort of reminded me of us? Three very different animals that somehow really got along? Well, since I knew that, in addition to being a real artist, Connor also designs commercial logos, I asked him to design a special chimera, just for The Three Investigators. I thought we could use it on our website, along with the question marks, and maybe also put little chimera stickers on the bottom of our cards."

Pete stopped and looked at them hopefully.

"What do you think?" he asked.

"I think it's a great idea," Bob said.

"Absolutely superb," Jupiter said – and he meant it.

"Really?" Pete said.

"Superpowers are everywhere these days and, of course, we all know there's no such thing," Jupiter said. "But the tradition of totem animals within some Native American tribes is worthy of emulation."

"That's just what *I* thought!" Pete exclaimed. "When we were in Yosemite and a golden eagle flew over our heads, right away it reminded me of you. Remember? I said you were like a giant bird flying over the earth, looking down at it."

"That's right!" Bob said. "I do remember. And I said that golden eagles saw things that other creatures failed to see. Just like Jupe. And they've got just gigantic wingspans – like the dragon on the decal. On the logo, the golden eagle's wings could be spread over the rest of the chimera."

Jupiter felt flattered by his friends' enthusiasm, but to his surprise, he also found that he connected to the vision they were promoting. In his mind's eye he was riding the thermals, alone and self-contained, looking down on the earth from a great height. He had a fellow feeling for a creature seeing the world at some remove. Pete's intuition had been sharp, and Jupiter accepted his kinship with the eagle. Nevertheless, he felt he should demur.

"Bob," Jupiter said. "You give me too much credit."

"Not at all!" Pete said. "It's perfect. And Bob − . Well, I said it first as a joke, but the more I think about it, the better it seems. Bob should be a bobcat."

Jupiter laughed.

"No, really," Pete said enthusiastically. "Like the lion on the decal. I see the bobcat on the logo as the body of the chimera, and that makes sense. Bob is so levelheaded and dependable, he's like the solid center of The Three Investigators."

"That's very true, Pete," Jupiter said. "An excellent idea. But better still, bobcats are known for their stealth and patience; they stalk and then they pounce. I'm always so impressed with Bob's research — the way he takes all the time he needs to find out the things he's looking for. Only then does he act. And like the bobcat, Bob's extremely adaptable."

"Oh, come on," Bob said. Jupiter could see the embarrassment had shifted to him, but he could also see Bob's pleasure. Finally he grinned.

"You know," he said, "the day Pete and I went to the Animal Rescue Center and saw a baby bobcat, I thought that sometimes I wouldn't mind being a bobcat myself. But what about you, Pete? What animal would suit you?"

"I couldn't think of one," Pete said. "So I asked Connor to just use a bighorn sheep. Like the one on the decal. He said he wanted to do a sketch and let us see it, so we can decide what we want to put in its place. He's going to attach it to an e-mail. Do you want to check?"

Jupiter leaned forward and booted up the firm's computer. Sure enough, there was an e-mail from Connor O'Malley — and attached to it was a JPG, which Jupiter opened.

Although Jupiter knew that Connor was

an excellent artist, he was still extremely impressed by the sight which met his eyes – important elements of a golden eagle, a bobcat, and a bighorn sheep combined into one colorful and dramatic animal.

"Wow!" said Pete. "That's fantastic!"

"I love it!" said Bob. "And those bighorn horns! A bighorn sheep is perfect as the third animal. "

"I think you're right, Bob," Jupiter said. "Although many varieties of sheep have been domesticated, bighorn sheep are still wild. And the rams are fearless – leaping around the mountains from crag to crag, plunging into battle. They don't back down. They have the warrior spirit."

"Also, bighorn sheep are native to North America," Bob said. "Golden eagles are found elsewhere, but bobcats and bighorn sheep are only found here. That would make our symbol very American."

For a moment, Pete still looked a little uncertain, but he also looked persuadable, Jupiter saw.

Pete said, "Well, I *do* like those horns, actually, but this really *was* supposed to be just a preliminary sketch."

"As far as I'm concerned, it's the final

one," Bob said.

Pete hesitated a moment longer, then said, "All right! I'll *be* the bighorn sheep! As long as I'm not the goat!"

At that moment, the intercom that connected Headquarters to the Salvage Yard squawked and Aunt Mathilda's unnaturally amplified voice filled the room.

"Are you in there with the boys, Jupiter?" Aunt Mathilda said. "I see their bikes out here."

Jupiter pressed the TALK button. "Yes," Jupiter said. "We're all here."

"Then the three of you should get out here right away," Aunt Mathilda said. "An old friend of yours wants to speak with you." The electric hum of the intercom abruptly stopped.

"Who could that be?" Pete asked. "Mallory?"

"No," Bob said. "She's a new friend. Worthington?"

"If it were Worthington, Aunt Mathilda would have said so," Jupiter said. He slipped the counterfeit bills back in their envelope and returned the envelope to the drawer, then led the way out of Easy Three.

Once the boys had cleared their outside workshop, they could see the Rocky Beach police chief, Chief Reynolds, standing next to his cruiser, talking with Jupiter's aunt. In the years since the boys had first met him, Chief Reynolds's hair had begun to gray, but, aside from his limp, he still resembled the high school and college athlete whose slide into third base had ended his athletic career. He was lanky, easygoing, and cheerful.

"Hey, Chief!" Pete called. "Good to see you!"

When Aunt Mathilda saw the boys coming, she waved and went back into the Salvage Yard's office.

"How's everything at the Animal Rescue Center?" the chief asked Pete after the boys reached him.

"Great," Pete said, "though I'm just getting back to work there. We've been away for a while."

"You don't say," Chief Reynolds said with a smile.

Jupiter sensed the chief already knew about the events up in Jackson.

"You boys keep very busy," Chief Reynolds said. "The last time I saw the three of you, you were tackling that crazy bear-doctor. I hardly have time to turn around and you've finished another case."

"How do you know that?" Jupiter asked.

"I got a call from Jackson," Chief Reynolds said. "The chief up there and I have known each other for years. It seems you caught a big-time counterfeiter. Maybe you should come work for me!"

"That's kind of you, Chief," Jupiter said, "but we're already junior deputies."

Chief Reynolds laughed. "Then we need to upgrade your status." He turned his attention to Bob. "I know Pete's all set to play soccer in the fall," he said. "What sport are you aiming for, Bob?"

At Rocky Beach High, all students participated in some sport or physical activity. Jupiter had thought about this issue a good deal and still had not decided what he would do. Bob, though, apparently had.

"I thought I might try rock climbing," Bob said. "There's a climbing wall at the high school, and it seems to be pretty popular. Although actually, I'd rather climb on a real rock cliff."

"That's getting back on the horse," the chief said. Jupiter knew he was referring to an accident Bob had had some years ago when he'd fallen and badly broken his leg while climbing by himself on a nearby hill.

"And you?" Chief Reynolds asked Jupiter.

"I'm not sure," he said. He squinted at the chief. "I know you're a busy man, chief. Something tells me you didn't come here to check up on our athletic plans."

Chief Reynolds laughed. "Perceptive as always, Jupiter. The chief in Jackson faxed me a form the Secret Service wants you to sign. For their files. Just so they can tie everything up with a bow. In their typical manner, the Feds got in touch with the Jackson police only after you boys had already left Jackson. It's pretty straightforward, anyway. Just asking you to swear that you've handed everything connected to the case over to the Secret Service. They want to know, I guess, that you didn't keep any of the counterfeit money."

He laughed. "I understand that your newly-discovered grandfather was somehow mixed up in all this."

"Yes," Jupiter said. "But there were extenuating circumstances."

"Congratulations, by the way, on locating all those long-lost relatives," the Chief added, more seriously, while he handed a clipboard to Jupiter with the form. It was in triplicate; it seemed the chief had a machine that could print it that way. One copy for the Secret Service, one for Chief Reynolds, and one for The Three Investigators. Jupiter quickly read the form. It was just as the chief had described.

"Do we all need to sign?" Jupiter asked.

"No," the chief said. "Your signature on behalf of the firm will be sufficient."

Jupiter took the pen the chief offered and signed his name. He handed the clipboard back to the chief, who tore off the third copy on light blue paper and handed it to Jupiter.

"Thanks, boys," he said. "Always a pleasure." He tipped his cap, got into his cruiser, and glided out of the Salvage Yard.

Pete glanced at his watch. "Jeez," he said. "I'd better get out of here, too. I'm due at the Animal Rescue Center."

"Me too," Bob said. "Miss Bennett's expecting me at the library, and after that, I'm going home to start writing up my case notes."

"Have you decided on a title yet?" Jupiter asked.

"I thought you'd decided on *The Mystery of the Corlinagenous Colo*," Pete said.

"Not this time," Bob said. "That seemingly endless supply of phony money Michael Ivan was pushing into the banking pipeline up in Jackson made me realize I'd never really thought about money much − where it comes from and what it means and what gives it value. But in the last four weeks we discovered that real, solid, actual gold in the library, and then a barrel full of funny money − worth no more than the paper it was printed on. The two things together − along with talks we had about inflation − really brought home to me that everything has limits and there isn't a horn of plenty in real life.

"And 'chimeric' doesn't just refer to Pete's super idea," Bob added. "It also means 'hoped for but impossible to achieve' − like the horn of plenty itself. Even though you see the cornucopia everywhere at Thanksgiving − and that railroad used it in the advertisement Mallory gave us − there isn't an endless supply of anything on earth. So I thought I'd call the case *The Mystery of the Chimeric Cornucopia.*"

Bob looked a little breathless, Jupiter thought, and just a touch apprehensive.

Mallory's gift to The Three Investigators was leaning against the wall back in Headquarters. As Jupiter thought of it, he was struck again by what a great gift it was. He felt sure she saw the same illusory promise he did in its rich saturated colors and exclamatory lettering. He really did like it − and he really did like *her*, too.

"It's a truly ingenious title," Jupiter said.

"I like it a lot!" said Pete.

"Thanks," Bob said. He was clearly both relieved and pleased. "And it doesn't have to apply just to money. It can apply to anything you think will never stop coming. There's never an endless supply of anything — except for feelings. Every time you have one of those, another one is right around the corner."

That was true, as well, Jupiter thought. If he'd ever been in doubt about it, the past six days had shown him otherwise.

"Another case brought to a most satisfactory conclusion," Jupiter said. "Two cases, actually. And speaking of which — ." He took a deep breath and looked at Bob and Pete. "This all began, as you'll remember, just eight or nine days ago, right here, in the Salvage Yard. I had ink on the bottom of my foot — ."

Pete laughed. "And I said Bob and I stood ready to investigate anything. Particularly the mystery of you. And now it's solved. You're no longer a puzzle, a riddle, and a conundrum."

"I wouldn't say that," Bob said.

"No," Pete admitted, "I guess I wouldn't say that either." He grinned.

"Anyway," Jupiter said, "these sorts of things are hard to talk about. For me, at least. But I wanted to thank the two of you for helping me find what Chief Reynolds called my long-lost relatives."

"I'm really glad it worked out," Bob said. "Knowing where you came from is important."

"But I didn't want the two of you to think," Jupiter said, "that just because –."

"Are you kidding?" Pete said. "We wouldn't ever think that. It's cool that you've got Harper and Luke and Dora and John Pelletier in your life now. And anyway, we've *all* got two new friends in Branko and Mallory."

Jupiter was a little surprised to find that he didn't disagree with Pete's second sentence, and he felt grateful that he'd been interrupted at the crucial instant, so that he hadn't had to actually say whatever he would have said. Something about Bob and Pete being as much his family as any family he might ever have.

As it was, he simply nodded seriously. "Well, I'd better go close up Headquarters. Congratulations again on your great idea," he said to Pete – only to see Pete blush. Pete blushed more than anyone else he knew, Jupiter thought. In fact, you could add Pete's blushes to the list of things that *did* keep coming.

He watched as Pete buckled on his blue helmet, Bob buckled on his green one, and the two of them rode away from the Salvage Yard together. Then he turned and walked back across the gravel lot, through Easy Three and into Headquarters, carrying the sheet of paper Chief Reynolds had given him. Now that he was alone, he wanted to read what he'd signed more carefully.

He set the piece of paper on the desk, sat down, and opened the drawer into which he had slipped the envelope containing the counterfeit money. His eye fell on the piece of construction paper bearing his right footprint, and also on his birth certificate. He hadn't yet given it back to his uncle to return to the safe deposit box, and now he lifted it out and set it beside the form from the Secret Service.

It was interesting to consider that this case had begun and ended with official documents – first the Canadian birth certificate with his baby footprints, and now the Secret Service declaration. He looked from one to the other, then re-read the exact wording of the paper he'd let Chief Reynolds carry away with him. He found what he'd already suspected – that he'd signed a statement affirming that he and

Bob and Pete had handed over everything they'd ever had which had once belonged to André Laurent.

Strictly speaking, that wasn't true, of course. As Jupiter pulled the envelope with the five counterfeit bills out of the drawer again and set them beside his birth certificate and the attestation sheet, he remembered that some of the bad guys The Three Investigators had run into in the past had said that Jupiter would make an excellent master criminal.

Although having signed off on a statement that wasn't true in its entirety would hardly be proof of *that*, as Jupiter held the counterfeit bills in his hand, he found himself thinking about his grandfather, Spiridon Markovic. What had happened to vineyard owners like his grandfather really wasn't fair, and all of a sudden it occurred to Jupiter – maybe for the first time in his life – that even though the Founding Fathers had tried their best to devise a form of government that would permit the citizens who lived under it to use their lives and their liberty to pursue an elusive happiness, America had a lot of problems.

All countries did, Jupiter realized, but in a country that had acted as a magnet, for the last two hundred or so years, for people from all over the planet who were seeking freedom to build their own lives, it might be sadder than in some others when the government devised policies that made it either hard or impossible for a person like Spiridon Markovic to protect what he had earned and saved.

Up until the moment Jupiter's grandfather had run into trouble with his bank loan, he had thought that America was a place of both security and opportunity, and although some people might think that there had been no excuse for what he had done — and perhaps especially no excuse for secretly printing two million counterfeit dollars to try to run away on — the rampant inflation of the era in which he had lived had clearly pushed him in the direction of criminality.

In addition, when Jupiter considered that his grandfather had died of a heart attack trying to protect his wife and daughter from André Laurent, he found himself understanding Spiridon Markovic's motives remarkably well. After all, when André Laurent had taken Pete as a prisoner in his own car, he and Bob would have done anything — legal or illegal — to get Pete safely back again.

As Jupiter sat thinking, he'd been holding one of the counterfeit bills, and now he picked

up his magnifying glass and looked through it –
impressed once more with André Laurent's
murdered partner's preternatural skill. It was a
work of art.

By now, the engraved plates had probably been destroyed, but he would keep these
five bills as his own private memento. Something to remind him that life was a complicated
business, and that if The Three Investigators
were going to stay true to their motto "We Investigate Anything," they were going to need to
remember that "anything" included shades of
good and bad and right and wrong.

Nevertheless, he thought, while the bills
were safe in his hands, they might not be safe
in someone else's. He took a ball-point pen and
carefully, on the left-hand side – trying as much
as possible not to mess with the engraving – he
wrote the word COUNTERFEIT on each of the
bills, then tucked them back into the envelope
and put them in his special drawer.

When he sat back in his chair, he found
himself looking again at the advertisement for
California that Mallory had given The Three
Investigators the day they returned from Jackson. While fruit and flowers cascaded from the
straw horn, it wasn't fruit the cornucopia
promised but plenty, and plenty of plenty – in-

cluding plenty of money!

Just as Bob had pointed out, the core fantasy of a cornucopia was that life spilled forth unimpeded and full of certainties. But there was no such thing as a certainty in this life, and working hard wasn't enough to keep you or the people you loved safe. Since Jupiter and Mallory had both lost their fathers young, they both knew – better than most people their age, perhaps – that although you had to move forward into the future, you should never forget who you were and where you'd come from.

It had been a while since Jupiter had left Headquarters by any exit other than Easy Three, but after he had slipped the counterfeit money into its envelope, then placed the envelope, his birth certificate, and the Secret Service form back in the drawer on top of his inky footprint, he found himself looking up at Emergency One – a trapdoor in the mobile home's roof which led to a long curved playground slide.

When he and Pete and Bob had first constructed this emergency exit, they'd been younger and smaller, but although they'd grown a lot since then, a recent inspection of the slide had confirmed they would still fit under the I-beam that jutted across it halfway down. The Three Investigators had put the I-beam there to keep any adults who might try to follow them from being able to do so safely. Now *they* were the adults − or almost. But not quite.

Jupiter climbed on the desk, flipped open the trapdoor, and pulled himself through. He surveyed the Salvage Yard to make sure no one was looking, then stretched his arms over his head. He positioned himself at the end of the slide, lay flat, let go, and immediately gained momentum. He rocketed down the slide and flew under the I-beam, landing in an old bed of sawdust.

There, he lay on his back for a while, smiling with satisfaction, and looking up at a sky in which, if it had been evening, he might have seen the planet Jupiter.

ABOUT THE AUTHORS

Elizabeth Arthur

Elizabeth was born on November 15, 1953 in New York City. She is the daughter of Robert Arthur, the creator of The Three Investigators series. She was educated at Concord Academy in Concord, Massachusetts, the University of Michigan in Ann Arbor, Michigan, Notre Dame University of Nelson, British Columbia, and the University of Victoria in Victoria, British Columbia.

Before she started working on the New Three Investigators series in December of 2018, Elizabeth spent most of her life writing for adults. *Island Sojourn* – a memoir about building a house on a wilderness island in northern Canada – was published in 1980 by Harper and Row. A second memoir, *Looking For The Klondike Stone*, was published by Knopf in 1992. She is also the author of the novels *Beyond the Mountain, Bad Guys, Binding Spell, Antarctic Navigation,* and *Bring Deeps*.

Elizabeth's writing has received fellowships, grants, and awards from the Bread Loaf Writer's Conference, the Ossabaw Island Project, the Vermont Council on the Arts, and the

Indiana Arts Commission. She twice received fellowships from the National Endowment for the Arts and was the first novelist ever given an Antarctic Artists and Writers Operational Support Grant from the National Science Foundation.

Her novel *Antarctic Navigation* was chosen by the New York *Times* as a Notable Book, received a Critics' Choice Award from the San Francisco *Review of Books*, and was chosen as a Best Book of 1995 by *A Common Reader*. In 1996 the novel received the Ohioana Book Award for Fiction from the Ohioana Library Association.

Elizabeth has also taught creative writing at Miami University in Oxford, Ohio; the University of Cincinnati; and Indiana University/Purdue University of Indianapolis, where she directed the creative writing program. She and Steven Bauer met in 1980 at the Bread Loaf Writer's Conference and have been married since June of 1982.

Steven Bauer

Steven was born on September 10, 1948 in Newark, New Jersey. He was educated at Hanover Park High School in East Hanover, New Jersey, Trinity College in Hartford, Connecticut, and the University of Massachusetts in Amherst, Massachusetts. In 1970 he received a B.A. with Honors in English from Trinity, and in 1975 he received an M.F.A. in English from the University of Massachusetts.

Steven is the author of three books for young people – *Satyrday*, 1980; *The Strange and Wonderful Tale of Robert McDoodle*, 1999; and *A Cat of a Different Color*, 2000. His book of poems *Daylight Savings* was published by Gibbs Smith in 1989 and won the Peregrine Smith Poetry Prize.

Steven's work has received fellowships from the Bread Loaf Writer's Conference and the Fine Arts Work Center in Provincetown, Massachusetts. In addition, he has been given grants and awards from the American Library Association, the Parents' Choice Foundation, the Ossabaw Island Project, the Massachusetts Arts Council, and the Indiana Arts Commission.

From 1979 to 1982, Steven taught literature and creative writing at Colby College in Waterville, Maine. From 1982 to 2009 he taught at Miami University in Oxford, Ohio where he directed the graduate and under-graduate creative writing programs. In 2010 he established Hollow Tree Literary Services, an independent editing business.

www.ingramcontent.com/pod-product-compliance
Lightning Source LLC
Chambersburg PA
CBHW021027310726
48969CB00006B/1579